D0004784

Long Gone Daddy

Long Gone Daddy

Helen Hemphill

FRONT STREET
Asheville, North Carolina

For Jim Johnston

First Edition

Library of Congress Cataloging-in-Publication Data to come

FRONT STREET
An Imprint of Boyds Mills Press, Inc.
A Highlights Company

Long Gone Daddy

CHAPTER
1

The first time I met my grandfather, he was laid up on a porcelain prep table at the Hamilton-Johnston Funeral Home. His eyes were wide open and he had a grin on his face, but he was dead as a doornail.

His pupils were flat and unfocused and fully dilated, making fat, round black dots on the whites of his eyes. He had thin lips and a sharp nose, and his feet hung off the end of the table, so he must have been over six feet tall. His cotton pajamas skimmed his bluing fingers and toes.

I didn't favor him none. I took after my mother's side of the family with dark, scruffy hair, wild eyebrows, a weak chin, and a wiry body. If Elvis had married Jiminy Cricket, they might have ended up with a kid who looked like me. Only my mother said I was handsome. The guys at school called me Groucho. Or Blank Stank. Or sometimes PeeQ.

"Now Harlan Q, you don't need to be helping down here," Mr. Hamilton said. He nodded to me in the fluorescent light.

I had worked for Mr. Hamilton since last March, the day after I told Paps that I had given up on religion. That was four months ago; and as it happened, it was the very same day that Mr. Johnston run off with the funeral home beautician and twenty-two hundred dollars.

Good timing on my part, seeing as how Paps, who was the preacher of the Sunnyside Savior Church, didn't take to having a Doubting Thomas for a son. He made it clear that if I wanted to live in his house, I needed to find God pretty darn quick.

"I don't mind helping you, Mr. Hamilton," I said. "I never met the man. I mean, I don't feel sad or anything. I was just curious—what he looked like." I set the surgical needles and embalming fluid out on the counter. "Being kin and all."

"Naw, it just don't seem right embalming family," he said. "You go on upstairs now. I'll be fine."

"Where did you find him?" I asked. A blue tinge had settled along Grandfather's earlobes. "Paps always said that his old man left town twenty years ago, not long after Grandmother died in '52. He never heard from him."

"We got the ambulance run about two fifteen this morning." Mr. Hamilton took off his suit coat. He was a slight man but stood solid on his feet. "Heart attack at the Wayfarer Motel, Room 227."

"Does Paps know?"

"Probably. Sheriff Clambers would've called him from the Wayfarer. You might want to go over to see him, though."

About a week after I settled in with the Hamiltons, my mother sent a tin of Toll House cookies to celebrate my four-teenth birthday. Double chocolate chip with a cheerful card signed "Your loving mother, Josephine Pearl Stank." But I never heard from Paps.

"I guess I could."

"Well, get some breakfast, then get cleaned up and go on over," Mr. Hamilton said. "Isa Faye made rhubarb pancakes on account of the death and all. . . ." The sweet-scented aroma of pancakes coming from the kitchen would soon be overrun by the odor of body fluid and formaldehyde. The smells were my weakness in the funeral business.

Mr. Hamilton adjusted the water pressure. "I bet your daddy's wondering over why Harlan O came back to town. It's mighty sad they didn't get a chance to . . ." His voice died away, and two tears rolled down Mr. Hamilton's face in a full flood of sentimentality. Seemed kind of wasted on Paps.

Mr. Hamilton slid his hand over his cheek and then used his thumb and his index finger to close Grandfather's eyes. They popped open. "Just needs some eye caps," he said. "I'll get Harlan O fixed up real nice. He'll look like he's taking a peaceful nap."

Isa Faye called breakfast from the kitchen.

"Go on now. And tell your daddy he needs to make the arrangements."

"Yes, sir," I said. I took one last look at the remains. I could see some of Paps in my grandfather. Same hook nose. Same sandy red hair. But there was nothing special about him. Except that grin on his face. I kind of wanted to cry or something out of respect, but I was as dry-eyed as could be.

The smell of Isa Faye's good cooking won out over the formaldehyde. As I wandered into the kitchen, she flipped two toasted plate-sized rhubarb pancakes over on the griddle and pulled thick slices of bacon out of the frying pan with a long fork. They sizzled in the air.

"Here you go," she said. She took the syrup and drizzled two dotted eyes and a U-shaped smile right on top of the pancake stack. "I saw this on TV; they called it a happy face. Thought maybe you might need that today."

"Thanks, Isa Faye. But I'm not broke up or nothing."

"Well, eat up," she said. "You might feel gloomy later on and need a little smile."

I cut off a fist-sized piece of pancake and stuffed it in my mouth. There was only a half smile now. The syrup was warm and sugary.

Isa Faye's cooking was powerful. Rumor had it that her coconut-cream pie could make a man bawl like a baby. Once I asked her to make me one of those pies, but she said I wasn't old enough. Sometimes I dreamed about coconut.

"This sure is good," I said, my mouth about full.

Isa Faye wiped up the counter with a worn sponge and smiled at me. "Well, thank you, sir," she said.

I cut the other half of the happy face in two. "You knew my grandfather, didn't you? I mean, a little."

"Old Mr. Stank? Well, I was around him some when I was your age," she said. "I didn't really know him. I remember he could take a quarter out of your ear. Pull it right out from nowhere. That impressed most of us kids."

"I can do something better than that," I said. "I mean, not exactly that, but I have a trick I can do. The guys at school think it's pretty funny."

"I didn't know you knew any magic, Harlan," Isa Faye said.

"It's not magic. Kind of a trick."

"Is it funny?" she asked.

"Sometimes. The guys at school think it's real funny."

"Then show me!"

"I don't think you'd like it. Least not here."

"Oh, come on! What is it? What is it?"

I licked the fork again and tapped it against my front tooth. Sooner or later, I told Isa Faye most everything. It was some kind of spell she had on me. "I can puke. Anytime I want. On command."

"Oh Lawdy," Isa Faye said.

"I kind of twist my tongue around in the back of my throat until I start to gag. Then, nature takes over and that's all she wrote. I'll do it right now if you really want me to."

"No!" she said. "No, no, no!"

I teased her some more. "You sure?"

"No! I mean, yes!" she said. "Stop it! You're going to hurt yourself doing that."

"Don't hurt a bit," I said. "Natural as can be."

"Well, I don't want to see it!" Isa Faye said. "I'd rather you knew how to take a coin out of my ear. Why don't you work on that?"

I scraped up more syrup. "You think I'm like my grandfather?"

"I don't know," Isa Faye said. "You like to have fun, and he seemed like a fun-loving man. Smiled a lot."

"Why, he's smiling now," I said. "Got one hell of a grin on his face for a corpse."

Isa Faye frowned, but she wasn't really mad at me.

"Excuse my French," I said, hiding behind my milk glass. "Why do you think he came back?"

"It's a mystery," Isa Faye said. "Maybe he came back to see you, Harlan Q. I bet maybe he did, but his old heart just gave out. You know, there's a reason all this happened. I believe that with all my heart."

"Maybe," I said. "Maybe he missed Paps." I grinned and bit into a slice of bacon.

Isa Faye giggled.

"Or maybe he won the Publishers Clearing House Sweepstakes and wanted to make it up to Paps. 'Here's a million dollars, son. Now you can retire from that soul-saving drudgery every Sunday.'"

"You are just plumb shameful, Harlan Q."

"Maybe he was just tired out and needed a place to die," I said. "That was probably it. Probably had nothing to do with us at all."

"It does kind of give me the heebie-jeebies that he died in the motel the very night he came back home," Isa Faye said. She smiled a faint smile. "But it's going to be fine, Harlan Q. Remember that." Isa Faye had a goodness about her that grabbed you up and hugged you before you knew what happened.

"I know," I said. "I'm going to clean up and walk downtown now." But to tell the truth, I wanted to stay right there in that kitchen until Hell froze over. "Thanks for the pancakes."

I went upstairs and laid out my clothes. Considering the

events of the night, it would be right to show up all bathed and pretty. Maybe Mother would be glad to see me.

I scrubbed the inside of my ears, washed my hair, and poked a little file around the edges of my fingernails to get the dirt out. All dressed and combed, I figured I looked none the worse for wear. But a fidgety worry settled into my stomach, and I fiddled with the cowlick on the back of my head for ten minutes before I headed down the stairs and out the door.

The Sunnyside was a twenty-minute walk past Main Street. The church building was yellow brick with some of the most God-awful stained-glass windows anyone could imagine. They were violet colored, with emerald green crosses floating in the center of calla-lily borders. The porch up to the doorway was covered in green artificial turf grass, which reminded me of the Little Putt Golf Emporium where Paps, Mother, and I had once played putt-putt on a trip to Dallas. Paps beat me in sudden death.

By the time I got there, the back of my shirt was damp from the morning sun. I was late to the service, and Paps already had his suit jacket off and was full into preaching. I slipped into the back row and sat down.

The church was full of blue-haired women, worn-out old men, and families with crying babies. Old Man Tinker and his wife were right in the front row, across the aisle from Mother. A curly-headed toddler right in front of me was stomping all over his mother's lap. An old man who was sitting in front of me leaned over and offered the kid a LifeSaver candy, but the boy mistook the man's kindness for a game of peek-a-boo. That went on for an eternity until the old man got up to usher.

The toddler looked at me for a moment with gleeful eyes, but I snapped my head back to the pulpit and glued my gaze on Paps. Peek-a-boo could suck you in like a spider web. Babies and toddlers can keep at it for hours—until you beg for mercy, but there never is any. You'll be dead before a toddler will give up on peek-a-boo.

Paps roared in his preacher voice. "Men may walk into the valley of sin and sorrow, may test God's love and patience, may choose Hell and sin as a lifelong path, but they cannot escape the love of the Divine for His children. The devil never wins. Even when he walks among us!"

Paps posed for a second in front of the congregation, and an old woman yelled, "Amen!" She raised her hands in the air and waved them back and forth. Other hands popped up. Paps nodded in approval, closed his eyes, and waited. A second later, he was back to preaching, telling the whole congregation why they were a sorry lot of sinners.

All my life, Paps had preached to everyone about everything; he never gave it a rest. When Paps found out that the guys called me names, he marched right up to the principal during spaghetti night at the high school and carried on about throwing stones and loving thy neighbor. Rumor had it that I tattled to my daddy, but the fact is, I never said nothing. The guys were just having fun. No harm. No foul. But Paps's little sermon ended my social life.

The congregation stood for the benediction. Paps said the prayer. I thought about Grandfather dying alone on the tile floor of some motel bathroom. It was a sorry end for an old man. But he did have that grin on his face—like he was getting the last laugh. Was he?

CHAPTER

2

The service ended, and Paps walked down the aisle to the front door. He noticed me and nodded as he walked by. I nodded back, like I'd been to church every Sunday since the begats. He looked tired around the eyes, and in spite of myself, my heart stung a little for his loss.

Paps, known around the Creek as Reverend Harlan P. Stank, had been preaching and saving sinners at the Sunnyside with a full congregation and the blessing of the Southern Christian Convention since right after I was born. He had never mentioned Grandfather, but in an odd way, he hadn't forgotten him, either. Paps thought calling me Harlan Quinton Stank was just as natural as could be, notwithstanding the fact that Grandfather, he, and I would be named Harlan O, P, and Q. Every so often, somebody tells me it's plain weird. But now, after fourteen years of answering to Harlan Q, I have kind of gotten over it. Even weird things can seem normal if they're everyday.

Mother was across the sanctuary surrounded by a multitude of churchwomen. The minute she saw me, she fired a dazzling smile my way, then ditched the women and hurried over to me. Mother's smile could light up a football field. In high school, she had won Football Sweetheart, Prom Queen, and

Miss Bean's Creek, all in the same year, and still ended up a preacher's wife.

"Why you little stinker, sneaking in here like this. You look so good! I've missed the dickens out of you." Mother's eyes teared up as she shook my arm and leaned in to hug me. "I could just turn you over my knee for getting that job and leaving me like that." She kissed my cheek.

Pollyanna didn't hold nothing on Mother. She tried to find the good in everything and everybody. And when that didn't work, she just ignored the truth and made up stuff about people. Like my employment at the Hamilton-Johnston.

"How's Paps doing?" I asked.

"Sheriff Clambers came by about five this morning," she said. "It was just a shame that things happened like this. Just a crying shame. Harlan P was just commenting the other day that he needed to get things right with his daddy. But then, Harlan P never did have a clue where Harlan O was or what happened to him or anything."

Mother's dark hair was pulled up onto the back of her head, and she looked as fancy as somebody being interviewed on television. "Poor man. Harlan O must have been really distraught, or he would have kept up and told us where he was. It's just a shame." Mother drew a deep breath and fanned her cheek. "And Harlan P is always so busy with the church. It just wasn't God's will, I guess."

That fidgety feeling started creeping up, and blood pumped like crazy in the veins of my neck. I looked past Mother and tried to breathe out slow. Most of the sanctuary was empty now.

The usher collected Sunday service programs and wayward hymnals. A few people wandered about. Paps talked to Old Man and Old Lady Tinker.

I pictured Grandfather on the prep table at the Hamilton-Johnston, distraught in his pajamas and his smile. About now, his insides had been sucked out. I knew that feeling.

"I'm so glad you're here" Mother's voice chimed. "You look good. Just so good. The Hamiltons are being nice to my boy, I can see that." She pressed her hand to my cheek. "Did you get those Toll House cookies I baked for you? Did you notice they were double chocolate? Two bags of Toll House chocolate chips with just one batch of batter? I wasn't sure they would even hold together. Did you just eat them up?"

Out of the corner of my eye, I spied Paps shaking hands with the last sinning holdouts of the congregation. The Tinkers had left. I looked his way and slipped my arm around Mother's waist, gently pushing her toward the door.

Paps stood up straight and tall as we approached. Last time we saw each other, I had punched out the wall of my bedroom. Maybe he was remembering that, too. "Son, it pleases me to see you in God's house."

"Hello, Paps." I reached out to shake his hand but pulled back. My hand was shaking for some crazy reason. "Just wanted to tell you that Harlan O is over at the Hamilton-Johnston, and he's getting the best care in the world. Mr. Hamilton is embalming the body himself. I thought you would want to know." Paps dipped his head but his eyes weren't listening. "Oh, and I'm sorry about your loss, sir," I said, wishing I had said that first thing.

Paps looked down at me and then reached up and flicked his thumb along the top of his ear. An old nervous habit. His eyes skipped down my face. "Well, we are not exactly sure just how much Harlan O's death was a loss, but it was sure a shock," Paps said. "No news in twenty years." Paps kept flicking. "And he shows up to die? The Lord moves in mysterious ways. Mysterious ways."

No kidding.

"Harlan Q's coming home for Sunday lunch, aren't you, dear?" Mother looked hopeful.

I didn't know what to do or say. Paps nodded again. He was still stuck in God's mystery.

"I thought maybe that, considering everything, that I might?" I stopped. I hadn't meant to ask a question. My voice was changing all over the place; I cleared my throat.

Paps patted me on the arm until it about hurt. "That would be good, Harlan Q," Paps said. "Harlan O might roast in damnation, but God brings a silver lining in everything. He sure does. He brought you back to church and the word of the Lord."

Paps was full of wishful thinking. "But I'm not here—" I said.

Mother interrupted. "I've got a nice rump roast with potato salad, and German chocolate cake with ice cream for dessert, if you're a good boy." She winked.

"Go on to the house with your mother. We just need to finish up," Paps said. He always spoke like there was two of him, but he was just talking about himself. It was confusing as hell.

"How about some nice fruit tea, too, Mother?" Paps said. "Harlan Quinton always liked your fruit tea."

"Did you?" Mother turned to me. "I never knew you liked my fruit tea. You never said, you little goose."

I lied. "Sure, I like it just fine," I said. I hated tea and orange juice and whatever else went into Mother's disgusting little drink doled out to old ladies and bridesmaids. I had never drunk one full glass of it in my entire life.

"Good. We will see you at the house, then," Paps said. His eyes narrowed just a little, and I felt my cowlick pop free and stand straight up.

"Okay," I said. "See you in a minute."

Mother's driving was nerve-racking. Even the short mile to the house seemed like an eternity of nearly missed mailboxes. I chewed my thumbnail and tried not to say anything. Of course, Mother talked the whole way.

The minute we got to the house, Breenie started yapping her head off. She was mother's longhaired rat terrier—not really a dog, more like a wind-up toy with a high-pitched bark and sharp little teeth that snarled into an old-hag smile. Breenie was as black as her disposition, but Mother scooped her up and nuzzled her into her cheek.

"Now, now, Breenie." Mother's voice was soft and musical. "You remember our Harlan Q." Breenie showed her teeth. "Harlan's come back to see you. Yes, he has!"

Breenie remembered me all right; I was the competition. A

low snarl rose from her belly, and she yapped one more note. Mother dropped Breenie into the back porch window seat.

"Come on in, honey," Mother said to me. "Make yourself at home."

I waited for a moment. Breenie jumped to the floor and followed Mother into the kitchen. Mother shook out an embroidered apron and tied it behind her waist, went to the kitchen sink, and flitted around to stir her fruit tea and reheat Sunday lunch. Breenie sat by the kitchen sink and watched my every move.

Nothing had changed at the house. Mother's collection of ceramic roosters stood silent in the breakfront, and a bowl of hard candy sat on the kitchen counter. The dining-room table was preset for lunch, which was the habit of a preacher's wife. Mother added a place setting and handed me a tall glass of fruit tea.

"Don't you want to go on back to your bedroom?" she asked. "It's all there, just like you left it. I mean, of course I washed the sheets, dusted the furniture, and mopped the floor, but . . ." Mother lowered her voice into a whisper. "There is still that place in the wall."

Mother pulled two Tupperware bowls and a roasting pan out of the refrigerator. "Mr. Bernice was visiting his sick daughter, and then we had Vacation Bible School, and the church deacons' retreat, and now this whole mess with Harlan O. The summer has just flown by. The deacons' retreat went real well. They forgave you totally. You want a taste of the potato salad?"

"I'll wait," I said. It kind of made me shudder to remember

all the anger of that day. How Paps screamed at me for doubting the Lord. How Paps slapped my smart mouth for trying to explain. How Paps said I mocked everything and didn't deserve God's love. How scared I was because I knew it was true. How could God love a screw-up like me?

"Mr. Bernice said he might be out this week to patch it up." Mother slid the roasting pan into the oven. "Go back to your room and look around. Lunch won't be too long."

"I guess I could take a look," I said. Curiosity consumed me pretty quick.

I slipped down the hall, and Breenie's red painted toenails tapped behind me. I opened the door to my bedroom. The doorjamb was still splintered. Nothing had been moved, but Mr. Clean had been there. The bed was made, the trash emptied, the shelves straightened, the hardwood floors waxed to a dull sheen.

My posters were gone, but the hole in the wall was still there. The studs peered through the opening of the broken Sheetrock. I had a nice right hook. Funny thing about it was I didn't exactly remember my fist going into the plasterboard. I didn't remember slamming my knuckles over and over and over into the drywall until it was my knuckles that shattered. I just remember hitchhiking along the highway, and Mr. Hamilton asking if I needed a ride and seeing my swollen hand, and the ice packs Isa Faye made long into the night, and the throbbing pain.

That pain went all the way up my arm until I thought my chest would split wide open, and it worried me still. Mr.

Hamilton said I should try not to dwell on it.

Old Man Tinker was to blame. He taught youth Sunday school and acted all buddy-buddy and cool. Knew what bands were on the radio. Told jokes about rabbis and priests and Barry Goldwater. He wore blue jeans to Sunday-night service one time. And even told us kids his high school nickname: T-bone.

He was probably way over thirty, but he acted like one of the guys. So in Sunday school, when old T-bone asked us to write down the names of the ten most important people in our lives, I tried to tell the truth. Why wouldn't I?

1. Jesus
2. Connie C.
3. The guys
4. Jimi Hendrix
5. Don Corleone—The Godfather
6. Eric Clapton when he played with Cream
7. Mother
8. Paps
9. Ginger from *Gilligan's Island*
10. Jesus

Then Mr. Tinker went around the room and asked us if Jesus was on our list and why.

"Sure, twice," I said. "He's number one and number ten."

Tinker looked at me and frowned in an odd way. "One and ten, Harlan Q?" he asked. A couple of straight-laced goody-goodies giggled. The boy next to me scooted his chair away.

"It kind of makes sense to me," I said. "I mean, don't you

think it's a little weird that two thousand years ago some poor carpenter who probably wasn't even very good at his job ends up saving the world?"

Mr. Tinker just stared at me.

"Maybe Jesus was just a regular guy," I said. "A good guy who did a bunch of cool stuff. But maybe not holy, or godly, or the savior of the whole wide universe. And in the end if everybody gets fooled, then old Jesus is a ten."

"Well, I didn't know you were our resident skeptic, Harlan Q. But you have Jesus first on your list, too," Tinker said. "What does that mean, young man?"

The whole class froze, looking down at the linoleum.

"It's insurance—just in case this whole New Testament thing works out. Then, I'd want Jesus number one, right here in my back pocket," I said. "If the Bible turns out to be true, you kind of want Jesus quarterbacking. So I put Him number one just in case."

Things pretty much went downhill from there. Tinker turned red as a devil and told me that I was in serious jeopardy of damnation and needed to hush right then and there. No one spoke to me for the rest of Sunday school.

By the time the 11:00 service started, T-bone had told Paps and every deacon at the Sunnyside about my little list. The deacons called Paps on the carpet right after church and questioned why he couldn't save his own son. What about the welfare of the congregation? Should they report the incident to the Southern Christian Convention?

We didn't even get to Sunday lunch before Paps came after

me. I tried to get away from him and slammed my bedroom door against his rage, but he broke the door and demanded that I look at him. I couldn't stand the letdown in his eyes. *Thou shalt not doubt.*

I wanted to slap it away. Punch its lights out. But I couldn't. So I punched the wall instead.

All because I doubted.

And I told the truth.

No good deed goes unpunished.

Just then, Breenie jumped on my pillow as if to let me know it was just a matter of time before this was her territory, and I about spilled my tea. I started to put the glass on the nightstand, but I didn't know if I would mess up everything, so I just held it and took one last look around. The posters were in the closet. A jagged edge ran across Jimi Hendrix's face. I shut the closet door and left everything like I found it.

When Paps came in, we sat down to eat. Breenie found her place under the table as Paps said grace. "Dear Lord, mighty Lord, all gracious Lord, thank You for this food we eat so that we might nourish our bodies. Thank You for sending Harlan O back to us and Harlan Q home. Harlan O is lost to us, but we praise You for helping Harlan Q to see his mistakes. We knew he would find Your presence and revel in the love of the Lord."

I squirmed in my chair, and the wood creaked in dissent. Paps paused for a moment, while I stared into my lap.

"We knew he would turn away from sin and be with us, saved in Your love. We knew he would find Your forgiveness.

Be with us, dear Lord, as we see Harlan O through his chosen destiny. Thank You, dear Lord, for the Sunnyside Savior Church and all the congregation. Thank You, dear Lord, for Mother and for all good, righteous women in the world. Amen."

"Amen," Mother said. She smiled in fretful anticipation and unfolded her napkin. From somewhere under Mother's chair, Breenie whined.

Paps and Mother looked at me to say something, but we sat with the blessing heavy in the air. My eyes locked on my glass. The taste of the fruit tea lingered way back in my throat.

"Please pass the rolls," I said.

Paps looked down at his plate, and Mother handed along the bread, tucked in a crisp, ironed napkin. I took a warm roll, broke it onto my plate, and tried to ignore Paps.

"Butter?" Mother asked.

Paps frowned. His hooknose hovered above his tight mouth to give his face a full, angry draw. "Mother, be careful," he said. He pushed his chair away from the table. "We may be having lunch with a heathen here."

I looked up at him. I tore another piece of roll between my teeth and chewed the dough. I hadn't been here thirty minutes and already Paps was stirring the pot. He just couldn't let things ride. Not even now. My throat was dry, but I ground the back of my teeth and swallowed hard. If I was headed to Hell anyway, I might as well do some name-calling of my own.

CHAPTER
3

But the roll lodged in my windpipe like a wad of mortician's putty. Breenie growled, then gave off a full bark attack of ear-splitting yaps. She ran in a counter-clockwise circle, then trotted under the lace curtains covering the window and jumped up to the low windowsill.

"Now, Breenie," Mother said.

I couldn't breathe. I tapped my chest to get Mother's attention, but she didn't look at me. I didn't even have enough air to cough; the bread was stuck tight.

Breenie ran back under Mother's chair, and the barking grew louder. Mother bent down to find the dog. "Breenie! Stop that now. Harlan doesn't like it when you get so excited," she said. A car engine hummed in the driveway for a moment, then a door slammed. Breenie's shrill voice filled the air, and Mother looked out the window. "Do we have company? Who on earth would be visiting at this time of day?"

My eyes watered. Breenie's painful yaps came in rapid-fire now.

Paps searched under the table for the dog. "Mother, this dog is starting to run this house, and we do not enjoy it one bit. Where is she? Breenie, settle down," Paps commanded. "Settle down." Paps clapped his hands.

Breenie howled like one of those opera singers on public television.

I felt woozy. I tried to drink some fruit tea, but the glass slipped out of my hand, teeter-tottered on the table for a second, and the tea rushed out in a big puddle onto my plate. A loud knock sounded on the back door.

"Get the door," Paps said. "Harlan Q, you knocked over your tea. What is wrong with you?"

I stood up and leaned over the table. My chair fell backward onto the floor. The bread knotted deeper into my throat.

"Well, you did call him a heathen, Harlan P. I don't think that was really a Christian thing to do, particularly during Sunday lunch," Mother said.

"We were only joking," Paps barked back.

Mother held open the curtain, and Breenie jumped into her arms. Breenie whimpered, and Mother looked out the window. "It's Sheriff Clambers. I wonder what he's here for?" The knocking grew louder. "I'll get a dish towel to clean up the fruit tea."

Finally, Mother turned to look at me. Tears were steaming down my face. "Oh, goodness gracious! He's choking, Harlan P! Slap him on the back. Hurry up!" Mother knelt and dropped Breenie to the floor.

Harlan P pounded his palm on my back, but the roll remained steadfast. Mother went to the door to get Sheriff Clambers.

"Lord have mercy! Harlan P, get out of my way," Sheriff Clambers yelled. He pushed my chair away with his knee, stood behind me, circled his arms around my rib cage, and squashed my ribs into his chest with a hard, full pulse. Air surged out of my lungs and the roll went flying with the force of a Phantom II rocket.

I collapsed against the sheriff.

"Josephine, can we have a glass of water here?" Sheriff Clambers asked. Paps sat my chair upright, and the sheriff eased me into the seat.

"Oh, goodness, goodness. Harlan Q, are you okay?" Mother poured a glass of water from the pitcher and handed it to me. I sipped the water, then set the glass on the table. I leaned forward with my elbows on my knees and breathed deeply.

The roll had landed under the dining-room buffet. Breenie dove under the buffet, sniffed it, and then scurried over and sniffed me. I wiped my running nose on my shirtsleeve and breathed deeply again.

Paps looked at me. "Are you all right?" He knelt down in front of my chair and closed his eyes. "Thank You, dear precious Lord, for saving Harlan Q. It was Your work that called Sheriff Clambers here to us just when we needed him. Praise Your holy ways, oh Lord, and keep Harlan Q safe all the days of his life. Amen."

"Amen," I said, too exhausted to care. "Amen. Amen. Amen."

Paps smiled and stood up.

"Amen!" Mother said. "Well, where are my manners? Sheriff Clambers, please join us for Sunday lunch. I've got German chocolate cake for dessert. I know how much you like it."

Sheriff Clambers grinned back at her, admitting his weakness. "Sure, Josephine. That would be fine. I brought some things of Harlan O's to give y'all. We can do that after we eat."

Paps nodded.

Within five minutes the table was reset, and we were eating. I didn't feel much like swallowing anything except mashed up potato salad and Mother's overcooked green beans. Sheriff Clambers ate plenty for both of us. After his second piece of cake, we got around to talking about Harlan O.

"His personal effects are in the squad car," said Sheriff Clambers. His spoon made a tinkling sound as he stirred cream into his coffee. "There weren't much, just some clothes and a few papers. But he was wearing a two-carat diamond ring, and there was a letter addressed to you, Harlan P."

"A letter?" Paps asked.

"Must have written it last night. On Wayfarer stationery."

"Do you know how he got to the Wayfarer?" Paps rested his elbow on the table and flicked his ear several times.

"A cab. All the way from Dallas Love Field, near as I can tell. Must have cost two hundred dollars or more. Maybe he wanted to surprise everybody." Sheriff Clambers pushed his chair back. "Let me run get everything so you can take a look. Coffee's a little too hot anyway. Be right back."

Breenie got up to follow him. "Stay, Breenie," Mother said. When Sheriff Clambers went outside, Mother put her hand to my cheek. "Feeling better?" she asked.

"Better, but still a little gaggy," I said.

Paps looked up. "We were just teasing you, you know. Never thought you were a heathen—not to the core. Not like that mischievous little dog sometimes. Now, she can be the devil." Paps pointed his spoon at Breenie.

The sheriff came back carrying a suitcase and a big envelope. "The suitcase is just clothes," he said. "You might want to look at this other stuff first." He laid a large, brown padded envelope on the table. "The ring is in there. And the letter. I opened it and read it; sorry, law enforcement procedures when there's a cadaver."

Paps opened the envelope and sorted through the odd papers and leftover ends of a lifetime. There was the ring. A book of matches. Some keys. And a receipt stub from Yellow Checker Cab Company. Grandfather's wallet had a wad of twenties, a couple of old business cards, and pictures of people we had never seen. "Looks like Harlan O lived in Nevada," Paps said.

Sheriff Clambers nodded. "Driver's license says Las Vegas. Could explain the diamond and the cash," he said.

I picked up the ring and polished it on my tie. It was the biggest diamond I had ever seen. "Do you imagine it's real?" I asked.

"Oh, let me see the diamond," Mother said. "My, it's a doozy, isn't it?" Breenie jumped into her lap.

"Now, Mother, we have no idea how Harlan O got that ring. It might very well be the benefit of some evil wrongdoings. Who knows what trouble my father found in Las Vegas?"

Mother tried on the ring anyway.

Paps picked up the letter addressed to him. "Read it to us, Harlan Q?" he said. "We need to close our eyes and fully concentrate." He passed the letter over to me.

I admit, I was mighty curious. The envelope was a plain white number ten marked with the Wayfarer's logo.

Sheriff Clambers cleared his throat. "I should be going, but I'll need you to sign a receipt," he said. "For the personal effects."

"Thank you for everything you did today," Paps said. "The Lord worked right through you today, and it was a blessing to us."

The sheriff nodded. "Happy to help," he said. He looked over at me. "I guess you're one less body for the Hamilton-Johnston. Hope Mr. Hamilton don't mind."

I smiled at his small joke. "Yeah, thanks, Sheriff."

"Obliged," he said. "See you around. And, sorry again about Harlan O." Mother scooped Breenie from her lap and held her while she walked the sheriff to the door.

Paps drank a sip of his coffee. "Well, open it," he said. Paps slid his chair back and closed his eyes. "I cannot imagine what he wants to tell us now."

I flipped back the open envelope and took out the letter and read aloud.

The letter was short and sweet, handwritten in a small, neat script.

Dear Son: I came here to see you and the boy, but now that I'm here it seems like a silly idea. It's been twenty years and about a lifetime since we last spoke. I've got a bad ticker, and I might not make it long. If something happens, call my attorney, Johnny Stiletto, in Las Vegas. He'll know what to do.—H. O.

Was I "the boy"? I didn't think Grandfather even knew I was born. Two phone numbers were written on the bottom of the page. Paps sat quiet and put his hand to his ear. Flicking.

Mother came back into the room hugging Breenie and admiring the diamond ring, which was now jammed on Breenie's front paw. Breenie held out the ring like she had just gotten engaged. I handed Mother the letter.

"Do you think Grandfather was in the Mob or something?" I asked. "A name like Johnny Stiletto sure seems funny for a lawyer."

"Very odd," Paps said. "We just pray that we do not get mixed up in something evil." More flicking.

"Well, at least Mr. Stiletto can tell us what all this mystery is about. That *is* an unusual name. Stiletto. Do you think he's American?" Mother said, prancing Breenie around in her lap.

"Only one way to find out," I said. "Let's call him. If he's some Mafia lawyer, he probably won't mind us calling him on Sunday. Probably gets emergency calls all the time."

Paps stopped flicking his ear. "Perhaps you are right, Harlan Q. We need to see what this is all about."

"Want me to make the call?" I asked.

"No, we can do this. We do not know this Mr. Stiletto. He

could be some lawless criminal set on doing evil in the world, and we need to be on our guard."

We? Paps was killing me here. Was he talking about himself and some angel in his pocket?

"Help your mother clean up," Paps said. "We will find out what is going on. And pray to the Lord that your grandfather did not end up in some compromising circumstance that will only break our hearts." Paps went into the living room and pulled the doors closed.

I squinted my eyes at the woodwork. "Be careful!" I said in a too loud voice. "You don't want them sucking your soul out through the telephone line!" Breenie barked, and I snarled back at her.

"Now, Harlan, be nice," Mother said.

"Why?" I asked. I frowned at Mother, too. She didn't tell *Breenie* to be nice.

I picked up the empty glasses on the table and set them near the sink in the kitchen. When I turned, the telephone caught the corner of my eye, and I was tempted. Old Moses never said, "Thou shalt not eavesdrop."

I rinsed out the glasses. I could hear odds and ends of Paps's conversation in the living room. I couldn't stand it. I carried the phone out into the hallway and eased the telephone receiver out of its cradle.

Paps's voice boomed into my ear. "The arrangements are not settled yet. We, uh, do not meet with the funeral home director until tomorrow."

I tried not to breathe into the phone.

"You planned to have the funeral there? In Texas? Without coming back to Las Vegas?" Mr. Stiletto's voice was a nervous tenor. He spoke fast. I already knew his eyes were shifty.

"Yes, that is our plan," Paps said.

"Can't do it. No sir. Not if you want the money. The funeral must be held here in Las Vegas. It's written in the will."

"The will?" Paps asked.

"You'll have to make arrangements to bring your father's remains to Las Vegas," Mr. Stiletto said. "We can administer the will while you're here. Won't take fifteen minutes. Your father left a sizeable inheritance, and we need to—"

"Did you say inheritance?"

"Fifty thousand dollars and change and a brand-spanking-new Eldorado convertible. Purple with a hell of a lot of chrome. Doesn't even have five thousand miles on it."

"Holy smokes!" I yelled. I slapped my hand over my mouth.

"Harlan Q, are you on the phone?" Paps bawled right into the receiver. "Are you listening in? Hang up that phone right now! Mr. Stiletto, excuse me for a moment."

Muffled words rang through the receiver in stereo as Paps's loud preacher voice boomed out from the living room. "Harlan Quinton Stank! You do not want me coming in that kitchen! Hang up the phone now!"

I slammed down the receiver. My God, we were rich!

That old coot. Grandfather was working for the Mob all the time. Maybe he was on the run. Or a hit man. I mean, I had seen *The Godfather* twice in the last month alone. I knew how it worked.

That's why Grandfather had the smile on his face. Cards. Whiskey. Showgirls. Grandfather was a trained professional sinner who had probably committed a whole collection of evils.

God did work in mysterious ways. Fifty thousand dollars and a new Eldorado just waiting for us in Las Vegas? Hallelujah in heaven! Why, if things kept going this good, I might have to tell old T-bone that Jesus had taken a permanent place at the top of my list.

An irritable shout vibrated out of the wall. "Harlan Q, get in here right now!" Paps was off the phone.

CHAPTER

"Do not be ridiculous! We are not burying Harlan O in Las Vegas!"

"Why not?" I said. I had decided to butt full ahead into Paps's business.

"You can't bury Grandfather here," I said. "Not now. We know he wanted to go back to Las Vegas. Mr. Stiletto said it was in the will. Way I see it, you don't have a choice."

"We always have a choice, Harlan Q. Whether it is to listen in on someone's private conversation or to give in to some silly request by a sick old man. There are always choices in this life, sir." Paps leaned his head back against his easy chair and closed his eyes. "Besides, it would cost a fortune to get Harlan O back to Nevada. We do not have that kind of money."

"But Grandfather is leaving you fifty thousand dollars and change," I said. "You could afford it. You could give Grandfather a simple graveside service right in the cemetery. Say a few words. Collect the money. And drive his Eldorado home."

"What if it is money made illegally, Harlan?" Paps's voice was stern. "We have no idea what kind of man my father was. That money could be the direct result of gambling or drinking or drugs. We do not have any idea what human suffering was caused to get hold of that money and that Cadillac."

"What would Grandfather think if we didn't take the money?" I didn't wait for Paps to answer. "Maybe it was his way of asking for forgiveness. Forgiveness money."

Paps reached for his Bible on the side table. "Harlan O is dead; whether his remains are buried here or there does not matter. It is just a body. We need to worry about his soul and salvation. We are not going to Las Vegas, and that is the end of it."

I let out a long breath. More than life itself, I wanted to go to Las Vegas. It wasn't really the money or Grandfather's Cadillac. It was the adventure I coveted. The action. I wanted to live a big old life like Grandfather had. It just didn't seem possible stuck here with Paps in pitiful old Bean's Creek.

Paps turned on the living-room radio, and we sat without talking. From the radio, Oral Roberts took an intermission from his sermon. The announcer came on asking for prayer requests and donations. Paps never looked up from his Bible.

On the radio an old guy called in for his sick wife's cancer. A woman wanted a new hot-water heater. A little kid with a lisp asked for an operation. All those people wanted was a couple of bucks and a little sympathy. I wanted a miracle.

Then, out of the blue, the idea struck me hard. Oral Roberts preached to desperate folks looking for salvation, just like Paps. And Paps would chomp at the bit to have thousands of sinners listen to him preach. Fifty thousand dollars could probably buy listeners—lots of listeners. "Praise the Lord!" I yelled.

Paps jumped back in his chair, like I had scared the life out of him.

I held my hand over my ear, like an announcer on TV. "*The Sunnyside Savior Church Radio Hour* with the Reverend Harlan P. Stank, direct from Bean's Creek, the heart and soul of north Texas."

"What?"

"Listen, Paps, I know you would never consider money that was received as a result of evil doings," I said. "It just wouldn't be right, with you a minister and all. I know that." I stopped for a moment and looked right in Paps's eyes. "But what if God wants you to have that money?"

I stood up and paced the floor. "What if God's saying, 'Harlan P, take that money and do good. Save souls and serve the Lord.'"

Paps sat up straight in his chair and studied me hard. He was thinking, all right.

"Listening to Oral Roberts just now, it just hit me like a bat out of the blue that you need your own radio show, Paps. I think God wants you to take Grandfather to Las Vegas, get that inheritance money, and start your very own radio revival, right over the airwaves. God's working through me, Paps! I feel it! I feel it!" I put my hands in the air like the "Amen" woman at the Sunnyside. Okay, so maybe I was playing it up a little.

Wheels turned behind Paps's eyes. He began to nod and flick his ear. "We like your idea, son!"

"Why, Paps, you could have church camps and summer tent sermons all over Texas. The Sunnyside deacons would love that."

"Yes, indeed!" Paps slapped his Bible shut. "Yes, indeed!"

"Reaching thousands of lost souls, waiting to be found. Waiting to give their lives to the Lord."

"Amen!" Paps shouted.

"Amen!" I said it like I really meant it, too.

"Well, God does work in mysterious ways. Praise the Lord. Praise the Lord, indeed, for working through Harlan Q."

I felt kind of proud to have Paps take to my idea so quick. That didn't happen a lot.

"We might best run over to see Mr. Hamilton," Paps said. "We need to find out some details before we get our hopes up." Paps picked up his jacket. "You want to ride over there?"

"Sure," I said. My stomach growled in excitement. On the way out, I kissed Mother good-bye and took some German chocolate cake for Mr. Hamilton and Isa Faye.

"Back to work so soon?" she said. Breenie started growling from under the kitchen table. I pounded hard on the tabletop, and Breenie tore out down the hall, yapping like a wild coyote. I escaped out the back door. Paps was already waiting for me in the car.

When we pulled up at the funeral home, Mr. Hamilton and Isa Faye came out and paid their respects. I was busting a gut to tell them everything, but Paps gave me a "settle down" look. Isa Faye gave me a hug and took the cake into the kitchen, while Mr. Hamilton walked us down into the prep room.

I folded back the sheet that covered Grandfather. "He looks good, don't he, Paps?" I said. Of course, Grandfather didn't look as fresh as he did that morning, but he was holding up. The grin was still frozen on his face. "He looks real natural, don't you think? Like he's just resting."

Paps frowned. "It is a pagan act to worship the shell of a dead body. My father is not asleep, and we should not deny the truth that his soul is probably lost to eternal damnation."

Mr. Hamilton raised his eyebrows at me. I guess neither one of us wanted to imagine old Grandfather burning in the pit of Hell.

Paps stood there silent for a long time, then said a prayer, but it was mostly about evil and darkness and sin. Grandfather smiled through it all.

I got a little choked up. Mr. Hamilton's eyes were watery, too. He folded the sheet back over Grandfather. For a moment, Las Vegas didn't seem so important. Sounds crazy, but I missed my grandfather. I missed knowing him something terrible.

We walked back to Mr. Hamilton's office, and Paps finally spilled the details of his conversation with Mr. Stiletto about Las Vegas. Of course, he left out the part about the inheritance. Paps could be coy with the truth as good as anybody.

Mr. Hamilton listened and wrote down some notes. Paps wanted the facts and figures—mostly the figures—on what it would take to get Grandfather buried in Las Vegas.

Mr. Hamilton punched some numbers into his adding machine. "Near as I can tell, it's going to cost about fifteen hundred dollars. You'll need to have a funeral home representative receive the body in Las Vegas."

"Some stranger will pick up Grandfather's body?" I asked. I didn't want Paps to send Grandfather back alone. And it wasn't just because I wanted to go to Las Vegas. I didn't want him to end up like a piece of freight. "Don't you think we should go with Grandfather?"

"I didn't include airfare for the family," Mr. Hamilton said. "That would be extra."

Paps nodded.

"And it doesn't include my fees for preparation and handling everything on this end." Mr. Hamilton tore off the adding machine tape and handed it to Paps.

Paps squinted to read the numbers. "Well, that is robbery, plain old highway robbery. No offense, Jake. But the Good Book knows all this funeral hoopla and la-di-da are all for show. Harlan O is dead and most likely in Hell."

Mr. Hamilton stayed calm. "Now, Harlan P, we're talking almost a thousand miles, and between the body and the casket and the permits . . ." His voice trailed off. "It's reasonable. Not cheap. But reasonable."

"Maybe this whole notion is silly. Seems the Lord is digging a well of an obstacle here. Just about closing the door on us."

I said the first thing that came to my head. "What if we drove Grandfather to Las Vegas?" I looked at Paps and then at Mr. Hamilton. "I mean, that way we'll know he got there safe and sound."

"Is there a law that says we have to fly the body out there?" Paps asked.

Mr. Hamilton leaned back in his chair. "No. No law that I know. Just got to have the death certificate and the proper paperwork."

Paps slapped the edge of Mr. Hamilton's desk. "God is

working through you, Harlan Q." His voice was fixed and clear. Well, we will drive it, then."

"We could use the station wagon," I said. "Drive the casket to Las Vegas, have the funeral service, finish up business with Mr. Stiletto, and drive home. No problem, right? Then Grandfather gets his burial." And I get to see Las Vegas—even if it meant going with Paps. But I didn't say that part.

Paps stood up and slapped me on the back. "The Lord's work is not easy, but we can do this. We do not mind a little driving for the Lord."

"Kind of unusual, but not illegal, I don't think," Mr. Hamilton said. "Harlan Q, you can handle the paperwork for me. I guess you could be the funeral home representative."

"Now wait, Jake," Paps said. "Harlan here had a good idea, but we do not think a boy needs to go all the way to Las Vegas. That town is dangerous, and we can handle it fine."

Every hope in my heart died. When Paps said *we*, he meant *he*. That damned angel.

"I don't think you should do this alone," Mr. Hamilton said.

"What makes you think for one minute we are alone?" Paps said. He was practically shouting now. "The Lord is right with us, Jake Hamilton."

"I meant, I think you should take Harlan," Mr. Hamilton said. "If something happens, he can help. He's been real good around here. Besides, don't you want the company?"

I stopped breathing. *Please God in Heaven, please let Paps say yes.*

"But Las Vegas is not the place to take a mere boy and—"

Paps stopped and looked over at me.

I stood up as straight as I could and gave Paps an encouraging look. "I'm not a kid anymore, Paps. Fulfilling Grandfather's dying wish means a lot to me. God's will and all . . ." I bit the edge of my lip. I wanted to go like an old dog with a small bladder, but I didn't want to appear too excited. Not with Paps.

He gave his ear a couple of flicks. He hesitated. I watched his eyes. "Well, maybe. I guess. But we cannot have any trouble."

"No trouble at all, Paps. Not a peep of trouble," I said.

He hugged me up to him. "Well, if the Lord wants you to be part of His divine plan to go to Las Vegas, we just have to respect the will of God."

I grinned like a kid on Christmas morning. Mr. Hamilton smiled right back at me. I loved that man.

"Harlan Q, I'll show you what to do with the death certificate," he said, "and you can help me get the casket ready for the trip."

Paps began to pray. "Dear, gracious God, this is exactly Your plan to take my father home and to give the Sunnyside Savior a radio voice to spread Your word and witness to lost souls. Have mercy on Harlan O, and thank You, dear Lord, for working through Harlan Q to tell us Your plan. Thank You for bringing our boy back into the fold of the Almighty. Amen."

"Amen," Mr. Hamilton said. "Radio voice? What's that?"

Paps looked a little sheepish then. "Well, there were certain stipulations in Harlan O's will," he said. "An inheritance of fifty thousand dollars and his brand new Cadillac if my father is returned to Las Vegas for his burial. We intend to use the money to launch a bona fide radio mission."

"Well, I'll be," Mr. Hamilton said. "What are you going to do with the car?"

"Sell it," Paps said. "Make as much as we can for the radio show. Did you know Harlan Q brought us the idea of the radio show in the first place? It was God speaking directly to him. Right in his ear. That boy is a minister of the Lord, whether he knows it or not."

Mr. Hamilton's eyes reflected a kind of phony wonder. "God spoke to you? Do tell."

My face heated up good. He could see right through me.

"Praise the Lord, we have got us a mission, son," Paps said. "We need to call a few people. Mr. Stiletto, too. Remember this moment, Harlan Q. God is working through you, boy. God is working through you."

We walked Paps out the back door and waved as he swung the station wagon onto the blacktop. The sun fell pink into the horizon. I had never been anywhere, except to the state fair in Dallas. Now I was headed to Las Vegas.

"So the Sunnyside Savior radio show was your idea?" Mr. Hamilton said.

"It was just a suggestion."

Mr. Hamilton leaned against the porch rail. "Harlan, I've known your daddy since he was seven years old. Down deep, he's a good man. Don't have too much fun playing on his ego. I do think he loves you."

"I'll try to get along. I promise."

"Maybe this trip will be good for the two of you."

"Thanks for making everything work out, Mr. Hamilton. I'll do my best."

Mr. Hamilton watched the station wagon disappear down the road. "It's going to be interesting, that's for sure." He opened the back-door screen. "We'll talk about everything in the morning," he said and went on into the house.

I stood watching the horizon. He probably didn't know it, but Grandfather had come to Bean's Creek to be my savior. The Lord did work in mysterious ways. "Whoo-hoo!" I yelled into the air. "Las Vegas, here I come!"

CHAPTER

5

Three days passed before Mr. Hamilton finalized all the paper-work. Paps picked out a solid-oak casket and offered up a nice gray suit for Grandfather. The funeral arrangements in Las Vegas were set for that Sunday. Considering it was summer, the service would be closed casket.

Grandfather would be chauffeured in style in the back of a 1972 Chevrolet Townsman station wagon with a V-8 engine. Technically, the car belonged to the Sunnyside Savior; Paps used it on official church business. That vehicle was like a tank—solid and sturdy and slow, with practical extras like an automatic transmission, air conditioning, and a power rear window.

We varnished Grandfather's embalming incisions pretty regular to keep the stench down. Between the varnish and the formaldehyde, the smell was god-awful. On the third day, we packed Harlan O in a heavy-duty body bag and varnished the zipper shut.

"Open up that window there, will you?" Mr. Hamilton stuck his varnish brush in an old coffee can and washed his hands. "Right after lunch I need you to help me go over to the warehouse and get the casket. We'll take the hearse."

The warehouse was actually the Texas Mini-Storage on the

edge of town where Mr. Hamilton kept the casket inventory. I liked riding in the hearse. It had comfortable leather seats and a radio antenna that could catch rock-and-roll stations from Dallas.

Once, when Mr. Hamilton and I drove the fifteen miles to Savoy to collect an old woman from the nursing home, the guys at school recognized me as we drove back through downtown Bean's Creek. I couldn't help but wave, being there was a dead body in the back. Their jaws dropped about south of Abilene.

After lunch, we got Grandfather all settled in his casket, then we crated the whole thing up—Grandfather, casket and all, in quarter-inch plywood—to protect the casket, Mr. Hamilton said. We got a couple of men from the welding shop down the street to help us lift the whole thing on a roll-around gurney, and we were sweating by the time the box was set and tied down, ready to slide into the station wagon.

Paps came by late that afternoon, and we measured the wooden crate—seven feet, eight inches—just to make sure it would fit in the back of the station wagon. With the rear seats down, we had almost six inches of spare room. Everything was gung ho.

Paps took out the map and fingered over the marked route: Interstate 40 to Albuquerque and Flagstaff, then curling up Highway 93 to Las Vegas.

"We called a former church family—you remember the Cleavers? They graciously agreed to let us spend the night," said Paps.

How could I forget the Cleavers? They had a beautiful daughter, Connie, two years older than me, and a seven-year-old son. They had moved to Albuquerque from Bean's Creek last fall.

"That puts us in Las Vegas in plenty of time." Paps wasn't one to dillydally, that was for sure.

"I kind of wish we had more time in Las Vegas," I said. "Maybe see where Grandfather lived?"

"I do not want to idle away time in that godforsaken place," Paps said. "Besides, praise the Lord, there is lots of work to do to get ready for the radio show. We need to meet with that AM station manager in McKinney right after we get back. The deacons are very enthusiastic about all this! Very enthusiastic!"

The next morning, Isa Faye got up early and made coffee. It was still dark outside. Paps said we would get breakfast on the road. My suitcase was packed, and I was already dressed in an ironed shirt and mostly clean blue jeans. I ran a little spit along the back of my hair to tame the cowlick and went downstairs.

Isa Faye smiled from behind the rim of her coffee cup. "I put some things together for y'all," she said. "Just sandwiches for later." A small Styrofoam cooler sat on the counter. About that time we saw the station wagon's headlights turn into the driveway.

"You are too good to me, Isa Faye," I said, gulping down the rest of my coffee.

"Well, I guess I just have a thing for you, Harlan Q." Isa Faye winked. "Don't go telling Mr. Hamilton, now."

I got my suitcase from the back porch. Paps had on a

short-sleeved shirt and dress pants. His hair was combed into a perfect pompadour. "Praise the Lord for such a beautiful morning," he said.

We circled round the gurney and carefully rolled Grandfather's crate down the back ramp to the car while Isa Faye held the door.

"We are going to have good weather from here to Arizona," Paps said. "You know, we thought about Jesus in the desert this morning. And here we are going into the desert, just like our Savior."

Mr. Hamilton lifted up the end of the crate and motioned for Paps and me to slide our end into the station wagon.

Paps rattled on. "I know the Lord will test us, and we will have to be diligent and faithful to watch for his will, but we cannot tell you how alive we feel at this very moment. It is like the Lord is directing our every move."

Mr. Hamilton pushed the crate carefully into place, lifted up the tailgate, and clicked it shut. I opened the back door and wedged my suitcase next to Paps's.

Paps was still at it nonstop. "We are just so grateful to be on this journey. It is the beginning of something powerful. We can just feel it. Let us pray."

Mr. Hamilton and Isa Faye bowed their heads. I concentrated on the Chevrolet sign on the back of the station wagon.

"Dear God, great God, Father of all the heavens, keep us safe on our travels into the unknown desert. Help Harlan O to find his resting place in this world, and have mercy on his soul in Hell's damnation."

Isa Faye stole a look my way. Paps went on.

"Thank You, dear Lord, for this opportunity to witness Your gospel to the wicked and the depraved. And help us always to know Your will. Amen."

I made myself a mental note to check Paps's morning coffee consumption. He was a little more chipper than I could stand that early. After the prayer, we stood there for a moment, pausing for nothing in particular.

"Well, give me a hug, Harlan." Isa Faye patted me on the back. "Don't take any wooden nickels," she said.

"I won't."

Mr. Hamilton put his hand on my shoulder. "Have a safe trip, son," he said. "Call me collect if you have any problems."

Even though I was anxious to get going, I hated leaving Mr. Hamilton and Isa Faye.

"You'll do fine," Mr. Hamilton said.

"Thank you, sir."

Paps clapped his hands. "We need to get on the road, Harlan Q." Paps shook Mr. Hamilton's hand. "See you in less than a week, Lord willing."

"Travel safely," Mr. Hamilton said.

Paps jingled the car keys in his hand and opened the front door. Paps had a couple of Bibles wedged into the front seat for emergency Bible study, but that didn't keep me from feeling downright gleeful. We were on our way. I waved wildly out the window to Isa Faye and Mr. Hamilton as we drove down the street.

The sun was just coming up. Paps put the back window down an inch or so for circulation, and I turned on the radio.

"It's going to be a hot one in North Texas today," the radio announcer said. "Look for a high of ninety-five with southerly winds of eight to ten miles an hour."

"We need to go west on Highway 82 to Wichita Falls," Paps said. "Then, it is straight on 287 to Amarillo and Interstate 40." Paps patted my arm. "We are just so thankful to have you here, Harlan Q. By the way, your mother made some Toll House cookies for you. They are in a shirt box under the seat."

In the back, Grandfather's crate lulled into the rhythm of the Townsman and settled against my suitcase while I downed a whole chocolate-chip cookie, followed by two more. The radio played gospel music, and the sun peeked out orange along the mesquite trees. Up ahead, Las Vegas, fifty thousand dollars, and a new Eldorado convertible waited for us at Mr. Stiletto's office. I thought it was about the happiest day of my life.

CHAPTER

A loud bang jolted me wide-awake. In a sudden motion, the station wagon skidded sideways and fishtailed over the double-yellow line and back to the graveled shoulder. It was like one of those rides at Six Flags Over Texas. I bumped my head on the passenger window before I could get my feet up on the dashboard to steady myself.

"Lord, have mercy!" Paps yelled. He threw his arm over me and muscled the steering wheel with one hand to stop the skid, but before you could say the Lord's Prayer, the Townsman was halfway in a ditch.

"Are you okay?" Paps asked. He pulled my shoulders around to him and looked me over.

I rubbed the knot on my head. "Nothing broken," I said. "What happened?"

Paps ignored my question, squeezed my shoulder hard, and drew in a long breath.

I scrunched up my shoulder to hide a full-mouth yawn. My eyes watered. "What happened?" I asked again.

The color had come back to Paps's face. "Tire blew out, most likely," he said. "We need to take a look." Paps opened the car door and got out. I was on the low side of the ditch with a stuck car door, so I scooted out behind Paps.

The morning sun was about halfway up the sky, glaring down on the station wagon. The tire was flat, all right. A big gash ran all the way down the side of what was left of the right front tire, and the wheel rim was almost sitting on the ground. The whole car sat cockeyed in a low gully—there would be no way to get it out without a tow truck. Nothing seem damaged, but it wasn't going anywhere without some help.

Grandfather! I shaded my eyes with my hand and looked into the back passenger window. Grandfather's crate had shifted and now had my suitcase wedged firmly between it and the glass. Otherwise, it was fine.

"Well, here we are," Paps said.

Here was nowhere. We were off a two-lane highway next to an open pasture with a couple of rusted-out pump jacks and some old corrugated roof metal that was crumpled up like tinfoil. The road curved to a hill, topped by dried-out grass and an old Dairy Palace billboard without so much as an ounce of shade.

"Where are we, anyway?"

"Just west of Wichita Falls. The other side of Electra," Paps said. "We took the wrong cutoff, and we went through downtown about five miles ago. The 287 bypass is a few miles ahead, I think. That will get us back on track."

Great. Five miles from downtown nowhere.

"We just thank the Lord that no one was hurt." Paps clapped his hands. "Hallelujah, dear Father, that we were spared injury and pain. You kept us safe. Thank You. Thank You. Thank You. Amen."

I leaned against the back end of the station wagon. "Maybe a car will be along in a minute," I said, not that I believed it. "We can flag it down, and one of us can go for help."

"We can get the car out."

"You'll bend the wheel rim."

"There is still some tire there."

"No, there's not. Paps, I don't know a blamed thing about cars, but if you try to get that car out, you'll bend the wheel rim sure as we're standing here."

"Maybe not."

"Then why did you ask?" My voice pitched up in sheer frustration.

"You do not need to be so sharp with me, young man." Paps gave me a warning look, then poked at the tire.

"Suit yourself." I bent down and pulled a weed from the dirt.

Paps gave the tire a couple of jabs, then stood up. "We should try to ease it out, Harlan Q." He took out a white handkerchief from his pants pocket and wiped his hands. "We can push it back onto the shoulder, then put on the spare tire."

The spare tire sat up in a wheel well just to the right of Grandfather's crate. We could probably wiggle it out, but the jack was full-fledged underneath the box.

"How we going to get at the jack? We can't get Grandfather out of the way. He's too heavy."

Paps peered into the back window of the station wagon and pointed to the crate. "Maybe you could lift up one side.

Squeeze in and push up with your feet, while we pry open the storage door and get out the jack. You know, this might be a little test from the Lord, Harlan, and we have got to do His bidding."

"It won't work."

"Just give it a try."

"It won't work."

"Push as hard as you can. We have the might of the Lord supporting us. With Him all things are possible. We believe that with all our heart and soul."

We? Paps couldn't leave God out of nothing. "We?"

Paps straightened up. "The Lord is always with us, Harlan, in His omniscient grace. His will be done. We take comfort in that, son."

"Paps, why do you always talk about yourself like you've got some invisible sidekick? I mean, most people—most normal people—say *I* when they talk about themselves, not *we.*"

"Watch your mouth, Harlan," Paps said. "The Old Testament says honor thy father and mother."

"Why on earth do you say *we* when you really mean *I*?" I yelled. "There is no one here but me, Paps, and *I*—as in *I, me, alone, nobody here but me*—I hate it when you talk like that. You're not the king of England, for Christ's sake."

"Well, if *you* continue to take the Lord's name in vain, young man, *you* will find the taste of soap in your mouth faster than *you* can imagine."

I crossed my arms over my chest and stared at him. We stood there in a kind of Mexican standoff. Paps walked away from me to the front of the station wagon.

Finally, Paps wiped his mouth with his hand and spoke in an unhurried wooden voice that got louder with every word. "Well, *you*, sir, could squeeze in and push the crate up with your feet, while *I* open the storage door and get out the jack, so *we* can change the tire and get out of here!"

I rubbed the sweat out of my hair. Far off, a cicada rubbed out a chant in rhythm with an old oil pump jack. A little breeze caught the side of my face. There weren't exactly any cars zipping past us. The sun blasted down on the blacktop, and I imagined a faint whiff of formaldehyde in my nose.

It was either Paps's plan or walk the five miles back to town. "Okay," I said. Paps turned around to face me. "Okay, we'll give it a try. I apologize for being so cross."

Paps nodded and wiped his forehead with his handkerchief. "You are always forgiven, Harlan—always," Paps said. "You drive." He threw me the keys.

"I don't know how to drive."

"You know how to start the engine and put it in gear?"

"Sure, but . . ."

"Then you need to drive, unless you want to get out here and push."

Paps had a point. A strong girl could probably arm-wrestle me with her pinkie.

"Just take it easy, and back up slowly. Maybe a good hard push against the front bumper will get the car on the shoulder."

I sat behind the wheel and put the key in the ignition. After a sputter or two, I fired up the engine.

Paps stood in front of the car. "Put your foot on the brake, Harlan. Then make sure you put it in reverse before you give it any gas."

About the last thing I needed was to run over Paps and have to call Mr. Hamilton. I eased the gear into reverse and slipped my foot off the brake pedal onto the gas. Paps dug in and pushed the car as hard as he could.

"Give it a little more gas, Harlan."

I gunned it by accident, then slammed on the brakes. The car died.

"Easy!" Paps hollered. I cranked the key, and the engine turned over. He dug his feet into the grass to push again and leaned against the bumper. This time, I said a little prayer and eased my foot onto the gas pedal with the caution of a ninety-year-old lady.

The rear wheels spun, then grabbed. The wagon lurched backward and rolled up out of the ditch. I put my arm over the seat and turned to look behind me. The flat tire made an awful thud with every go-round, so I backed up at a snail's pace until the station wagon sat squarely on the pavement. By the time I came around, Paps was prodding at the wheel, and it looked fine. Must have been my good driving.

We walked around to the back and Paps opened the tailgate. I wedged myself between the side panel of the station wagon and the crate, with my knees about up to my ears.

"Give it a push with your legs on three, Harlan," Paps said. "If you can lift it up just a little, I think I can get the jack out.

Ready? One. Two. Three."

I threw all my weight into it, but the crate didn't budge.

"I'm not strong enough, Paps."

"Let me see if I can squeeze in there," Paps said. But he couldn't get his legs folded enough for his feet to rest on the side of the crate. He nudged the crate as far as he could with his arm and shoulder, but we still couldn't reach the jack.

Paps wiped his forehead with his handkerchief. His shirt was sweated through, but his hair was still picture perfect. "We are going to have to take the casket out of the car, Harlan."

"We'll never get it back in," I said. "I'm not strong enough to lift up that whole crate. We'll be stuck here with Grandfather's corpse on the side of the road."

Just then, an old pickup crested the hill and rumbled down the road toward us. It slowed, then did a U-turn and pulled in behind us. The pickup was rusted out with so many layers of paint, it looked tie-dyed. A shotgun hung in the back window. An ancient old man who looked frail enough to break eased out of the cab.

"How 'do," he said. "Y'all got a flat?" The man wore faded jeans and a white-and-brown-checked cowboy shirt. The band of his cowboy hat was stained a dirty yellow color and he smoked a fat, hand-rolled cigarette. His face reminded me of Popeye, only older. Much older.

Paps started in. "Praise the Lord for a Good Samaritan." Paps seized the man's wrinkled hand and gave it a shake. The guy wobbled like he might drop dead right there. "I am the Reverend Harlan P. Stank of the Sunnyside Savior Church in

Bean's Creek, about three hours west of here, and this is my son, Harlan Q."

"Nice to meet you, Reverend," the old man said. "Well, let's take a look." He walked around the car and checked out the flat. "Yep, it's as flat as can be. You can't fix a flat like that." The old man took a long drag on his cigarette and blew the smoke through his nostrils. "You got a spare?"

Paps hung on every word the old man said. "Well, sir, we do. But we cannot get to the jack."

The man wrinkled his forehead in concentration, flipped his hat back on his forehead, and looked in the back window of the station wagon. "Well, take out that big box, Sonny. You got to get to your jack."

"Clearly, Mr.——," Paps said. "I apologize. I did not catch your name, sir."

"I never gave it to you," the old man said. He flicked the cigarette into the dirt and rubbed out the fire with his boot. "You can call me Luther. Just Luther."

"You see, Mr. Luther, we cannot take the box out of the station wagon because it is too heavy," Paps said.

"What's in the box, Sonny?" Luther poked his head through the open window, but jerked back at once. "Why something's ripe in here," he said. "You got a dead body in that box?" He laughed at his joke.

"As a matter of fact we do," Paps said. "We are doing the Lord's work. The crate contains a casket and the remains of my late father, and we are taking him to Las Vegas."

The old man took a step away from Paps. His face was

about as white as Grandfather's had been that first morning on the prep table at the Hamilton-Johnston. "What the hell? You one of them cult people?" Luther began backing up toward his truck. If Luther hightailed it out of there, we were stuck.

I nudged Paps in the ribs, and gave out my best full-bellied cackle. "Oh, Paps, you're such a card! He's pulling your leg, Mr. Luther. Why, there's no body in there," I lied.

Luther scratched the side of his head.

"It's books. Living Bibles." I said. "Did you know they're the best-selling Bibles in the country? We're taking a shipment to a church in Las Vegas. Paps just thought it would be funny to put you on some. Right, Paps?" I only half sounded like one of those carny men at the state fair midway.

"I guess I left my egg sandwich on the dashboard. Sorry, it kind of stunk up the car." I opened the passenger door and pulled out the waxed-paper trash from the sandwiches I had eaten before the tire blew out.

The old man eyed Paps for a long moment, then broke out into a slow, gummy smile. "Phew, Sonny, you about had one on me." Luther took off his hat. "Course it's Bibles—you being a preacher. And you never cracked a smile. Hee hee hee." Luther's laughter gave way to a high-pitched wheeze. "Yes sir, you about had me."

Paps gave me his most evil eye. "Mr. Luther, God will not let me deceive you. The truth is my dead father's remains *are* in a casket sealed in that box, and we need to get this tire changed so we can get on to Las Vegas."

Luther's toothless grin played along the side of his mouth

while he elbowed me. "Hee hee hee. Your daddy is funnier than any of those boys on *The Tonight Show*. Maybe you ought to be on TV, Reverend. Ever thought about that?"

I didn't want Paps making any more confessions to Luther just now. I nudged old Luther right back and let my laughter die out. "Well, how do you suppose we're going to get this tire changed?" I asked.

Luther wiped his eyes. "There's an old boy about two or three miles back down the highway here that's got a tire shop. Right on the highway. He's got one of them hydraulic jacks on the back of his pickup. Probably cost you fifteen dollars, though."

"Could you give me a ride there?" I asked.

"Well, I wasn't headed that way," Luther said. He looked at Paps. "But I guess I could help you fellas out."

"Hallelujah!" Paps said. "Thank you, Mr. Luther. We will keep you in our prayers, sir." Paps handed me a twenty-dollar bill.

Luther blinked a couple of times. "Well, okay," he said. "If you think it will do any good." He put his cowboy hat back on. "Hop up in the back, Junior."

I walked behind the truck, climbed over the wheel well, and swung my legs over into a dirty pickup bed.

The old man couldn't drive any better than I could. He ground the truck's gears and pulled out onto the highway. The engine backfired twice. I hugged my knees, and the air blew hot up my shirtsleeves. Pretty soon Paps sank behind the crest of the hill.

I had already been in a ditch, broken two Commandments,

yelled at Paps, and was headed off to God-knows-where with a toothless cowboy. It wasn't a bad start.

CHAPTER

7

We pulled into the yard of a rundown house surrounded by tires and parts of dead cars. A tow truck sat behind the house, and another newer pickup was parked next to it. They were both newly washed and spotless.

"This is it," Luther shouted, banging his hand on the door of the tie-dyed truck. Luther licked the edge of a cigarette paper, then struck a match on the dashboard. "Might want to get a new tire if you're going all the way out West."

Luther inhaled a deep drag from his cigarette. "Go on now, Junior. He won't bite. Name's Jerome. Good luck. You ought to try and get your daddy in one of those lounge acts in Vegas. Make a lot more money than preaching."

"Thanks," I said. "I'll work on that."

Luther tipped his hat and ground the transmission into reverse.

I walked up to the porch, knocked on the door, and waited. Nobody answered. I knocked again louder. I could hear my own breathing.

Four or five minutes later, the door flew open. I was already off the porch and walking back to the road.

"Hello! I'm looking for Jerome." Of course, my voice cracked like Glenda the Good Witch.

Standing there was a pretty boy a few years older than me with hair down to his shoulders. He had on blue jeans and a Grateful Dead T-shirt with the sleeves cut out. A large tattoo resembling Chinese writing of some sort decorated the muscle of his left arm. From the looks of it, Mr. Grateful Dead could probably bench-press over three hundred.

"Jerome!" he yelled as loud as he could. I stepped back on the porch, and we eyed each other while I waited. He smiled. I didn't care much for his nice-guy attitude.

Finally, Jerome trotted down the hall. "Sorry, man, taking care of a little business, if you know what I mean." He fanned the front of his overalls and held out his hand to me to shake. "What can I do for you?"

I pumped his hand just once. It was damp. I hoped to hell that old Jerome washed his hands after his business. "Got a flat tire about three miles down the road," I said. "No jack." I didn't want to explain. "Need to get the spare on the car, and probably buy a new tire, too. Heard you could help."

"A service call is fifteen dollars up front," Jerome said. "What kind of car you got?"

"A '72 Chevrolet Townsman station wagon. Flat's on the right front wheel. My paps is down there with it." I handed him Paps's twenty-dollar bill.

Jerome turned to the boy. "Get that G7015 bias-ply out by the shed," he said. "You probably got a fifteen-inch rim?"

I shrugged. How would I know? The boy disappeared while Jerome tied his bootlaces, hunted for his keys, and tried on several versions of Texas Ranger baseball caps.

"You can ride with me," he said. "We'll have to get the spare on, then come back here to get the new tire on the wheel. Won't take two shakes."

I tagged along behind him to the back of the house. There was a jack in the pickup's bed and a fancy tailgate that lowered to the ground. The boy put a foot on the bumper and hoisted himself into the truck in one smooth motion. He wore sunglasses and looked like he was right out of the movie *Easy Rider*. All he needed was a chopper. I was about as jealous as an ugly stepsister.

I got in the cab of the truck. Jerome turned over the engine easily, and for a split second, Grandfather crossed my mind. I just hoped Paps wouldn't feel compelled to tell Jerome and Hollywood here what was in the box.

Paps sat on the hood of the station wagon as we drove up, drinking one of Isa Fay's Cokes and reading the Bible. Jerome drove past the station wagon, made a U-turn, and stomped on the brake. The spare was already out, sitting next to the flat. All the car windows were down. That was a bad sign.

"Well, I am about as happy to see you as I ever was to see a man. You did not know you were an angel of mercy, did you?" Introductions were made, and Paps shook Jerome's hand like Jerome was the prodigal son or something. I wasn't about to tell Paps that Jerome might lack something in the hand-washing department. Jerome just nodded. His ears were red hot, either from the heat of the day or from Paps's continuous good cheer—I couldn't tell.

"Yes, sir, we just thank the Lord that you are here to rescue us." Paps said. He gestured with his Bible. The boy had jacked up the car already and loosened the wheel nuts in about eight seconds. It was like we had our own racing pit crew.

"Paps, I told Jerome here that we need to buy a tire. We can't drive to Las Vegas on the spare," I said.

"You headed to Las Vegas?" It was the first comment to come out of the boy's mouth. "I'm heading to Los Angeles myself. Going to work on the soap operas." He tightened the spare wheel into place. "Ran out of money, so I'm working for Jerome here."

"Jerome seems to be the gracious Samaritan to us all," Paps said.

Jerome handed Paps five dollars change. "You can just follow me up to the house. Your son knows the way."

I liked old Jerome. He did his job and kept his mouth shut, even with Paps singing his praises.

The boy rolled the jack out from under the car. "You want me to throw that tire rim in the back?" he asked.

"That's okay," I said. "We got a lot of stuff back there." He started to poke his nose in the station wagon. "What are you going to do on the soap operas?" I asked, not that I cared a lick. I just wanted him to mind his own business.

"I'm an actor," he said. "Don't I *look* like an actor?"

"Hard to say," I said. "Never seen one in person."

"Well, you're looking at one now. What did you say your name was?"

"Harlan Q."

"Unusual name—Harlan Q. I'm Warrior."

"They call you War for short?"

"Hey, man, take a deep breath," Warrior said. "Your energy is going all negative." Warrior kind of punched my arm, like we were buddies. "See you back at the house."

It took about every ounce of strength I had to heave the blown tire and wheel into the back of the station wagon. I wiped my hands on my jeans and opened the passenger door. Paps already had the air-conditioner going. The car smelled. Not a dead-old-man smell—more like a closed-up junior-high locker. I sat in the front seat, and we left the back windows down.

"The Lord is with us every minute, Harlan," Paps said. "We are back on the road, almost ready to resume the Lord's work." He pulled out to follow Jerome's truck. Warrior waved to us from the back.

"I think it would be a good idea to skip any talk about what's in the crate. These people seem a little oddball to me," I said. "I mean the guy's named Warrior. Don't you think that's weird?"

"I do not intend to lie, Harlan," Paps said. "Lying is a slippery slope. Once you start . . . "

"Well, tell the truth then," I said. "I'm sure that will win us a lot of friends."

Paps and I didn't speak the rest of the way to the house. When we got there, I hustled to get the tire out of the back and gave it to Jerome. "How long is this going to take?" I asked.

"About twenty minutes if everything goes right," Jerome said.

Paps and Jerome went around to the back shed to discuss the price. My hands were filthy, and I was starving. I pulled the ice chest out of the car. One last, limp ham sandwich hugged in plastic wrap floated in a slush of ice and water.

"Need some help?" Warrior asked.

"I've got it," I said, trying to be rude. "Thanks anyway." I leaned the ice chest against me and tried to wash my hands and face.

"You thirsty? I got a beer."

"I'm not old enough to drink beer."

"Says who? The Reverend? Don't limit yourself like that, man. Experience the world." Warrior turned and walked toward the house. My attempts to wash up weren't working, so I shoved the ice chest back into the station wagon and followed. Warrior kept talking, spouting off to himself. Somehow the whole conversation had turned from drinking beer to being happy.

"I mean, you've got to be happy, man. Even Buddha says that." Warrior chewed the earpiece of his sunglasses and looked at me like he expected an answer. I didn't have one. "Happiness is crucial to our souls, our very existence," he said. "So have a beer and be joyful, man."

What the hell did that mean? I was joyful. In fact, I was downright delirious.

"Can I borrow your restroom?" I asked. "I think I'd be real happy just to wash the grease off my hands right now."

Warrior ignored my little joke. "Come on in," he said. He took the back steps in one stride and opened the door. A TV blared out from the front room. "Bathroom's down the hall." Warrior pointed to the right. "Want that beer?"

"No thanks, I'm driving," I said.

"Uncola?" he said, popping the top of a 7Up.

I shook my head.

When I finished in the bathroom, Warrior was sitting cross-legged in the middle of the dining-room floor. Books were stacked neatly along the wall.

"Have a seat," Warrior said. "I've just started doing this whole meditation thing. When you came to the door, I hadn't finished my sequence. Give me a minute."

I found the lone chair in the room. Warrior had his eyes closed so I looked at the book titles. *I'm OK—You're OK. The Godfather. The Teachings of the Compassionate Buddha. Zen Mind, Beginner's Mind. Joy of Cooking.* There was also a Bible.

From deep in his throat, Warrior began to hum a low-pitched sound that went on for five minutes straight. *The Price Is Right* blasted out from the next room. Some lady tried to guess the price of Breck shampoo so she could win a bass boat. A dollar twenty-nine popped into my head. Those Breck girls couldn't be cheap.

Warrior spoke up in a loud voice. "It takes a long time to understand nothing," he said. "Empty your mind. Empty your mind." He hummed again in a higher voice that sounded a lot like Tiny Tim. That Warrior was one weird cat.

The woman won the boat. Eighty-nine cents. I picked at the carpet and waited.

Finally, Warrior breathed in and out slowly, like it was his last breath on earth. He reached for his 7Up. "I'm a PK, too," he said.

"PK too?"

"Preacher's kid," Warrior explained. "I ran away when I was about your age. I went back home, though—I was just a kid. Finally left again a couple of months ago. Just hitchhiked away one day."

Our eyes locked for a moment, but I looked away quick. "You've got lots of books," I said. "Saw that movie *The Godfather*. Snuck in to see it. Kind of nerve-racking." I scratched the back of my head. "But I bet the Mob is just like that."

"Man, it was unbelievable," Warrior said. "I would have been so good in that film. I mean, Al Pacino was all right, but I just keep seeing myself up there on the screen." Warrior turned and sat facing me. "Man, I just got to get to L.A. My career isn't exactly taking off with the Electra Community Theatre."

"So you read all these books?" I asked.

"Some of them," Warrior said. "I'm into this Zen thing now—the meditation? Like just being cool about everything. Dealing with what's right in front of you at the moment. Calm. Tranquil. Total Peace." Warrior laughed and gave me the peace sign. "So long as my lottery number is 347, I'm cool." Warrior's chuckle died out.

No wonder Warrior was all into *happy*. Maybe by the time I turned eighteen, the government would stop pulling birth dates out of a fishbowl to see who would have the joy of heading out to Vietnam.

"What's your tattoo?" I asked. "I mean, does it say something? Is it a picture of something?"

"Spells *Warrior* in Chinese." Warrior flexed his muscle to show off the black symbols. "You don't read Chinese from left to right like English, man. You read down, so the symbols mean *Warrior.*"

"Your mother name you Warrior?" I knew better.

"No, little one, my name is chosen from my inner strength and courage."

That shut me up. We didn't say another word until Paps and Jerome showed up. Twenty-seven dollars later, the new tire was all set, and the spare was back in the wheel well next to Grandfather. I was anxious to get going. Jerome offered Paps a drink of water while he searched for change for a fifty.

Paps looked around for a chair.

"Pull up a piece of floor, Reverend," Warrior said. He gave Paps his Hollywood smile. "So you're heading to Las Vegas?"

"Yes," Paps said. He leaned back into the wall and drank a long swallow of ice water. "Hope to be in Nevada sometime tomorrow night. I have an appointment regarding my father." Paps looked at me.

"Need another driver?" Warrior asked. "I mean, Harlan Q—it's Harlan Q right? He doesn't look old enough to drive. How old are you, anyway?" He didn't wait for me to answer. "Looks like this is one heck of a long trip for just one man at the wheel. I'm headed to L.A., but I could work in Vegas for a while before I head on out. I'd love to help you out, sir."

"I admit, this morning has taken it out of me," Paps said.

"But I cannot pay you, Mr. Warrior."

"Oh, I wouldn't charge you, Reverend. You need a driver; I need a ride. Seems like a fair trade."

I sat up. No way Paps would let some unknown Zen-practicing pretty boy drive the Townsman. What would happen if old Warrior here wrecked the station wagon and Grandfather ended up all over the interstate?

"You ever had a speeding ticket, son? Or a serious wreck?" Paps asked. I could have bet money that Warrior had a boatload of tickets. He was about as fast a hustler as I'd ever seen. Why was Paps even asking about tickets?

"Perfect driving record," Warrior said. "Just ask Jerome. He would never let me touch that tow truck if he thought for a minute I might wreck it."

"Well, we have some cargo in the back, so there will not be much room," Paps warned.

"I'll make do," Warrior said.

Paps had lost his mind.

"What is your real name, son? Can I see your driver's license?" Paps asked.

Warrior stood up and reached for his wallet. He handed the license over to Paps.

"Warren Ducklo. Ducklo—that is a familiar name for some reason," Paps said. "From Dallas?"

I laughed out loud. No wonder old Warren wanted to be called Warrior. Paps gave me a cross glance. "Have you met your Savior, Warren?"

"No sir, I haven't," Warren said, all sincere like. "I guess you could say I'm still searching."

"Paps, could I talk to you outside for a minute?" I asked. Had he forgot about Grandfather? We couldn't have Warrior all cozy with Grandfather in the back of the wagon. We didn't even know Warrior. I didn't trust that preacher's-kid-peace-love-dove thing for a minute.

Paps walked out onto the porch with me. "How exactly are you going to introduce Grandfather to old Warren?" I asked. My voice turned high pitched and hysterical. "Don't you think he'll wonder what's in the smelly box in the back?"

Paps's jaw turned to stone. "Harlan, you need to settle down. The fact is we cannot make it to Las Vegas by tomorrow night without some help here. You do not drive; Warren does. Besides, the Lord has offered us up a lamb, and we need to help him find his soul. If you were not so selfish sometimes, you might see that. Warren is going with us. We have made up our mind that it is the will of God." Paps turned and walked back into the house.

My throat slammed shut, and I couldn't breathe for nothing. Well, Paps could just break the news about Grandfather to Warren all by his lonesome. Warrior wouldn't be five miles down the road until he regretted this little setup.

I sat on the steps until Paps and Warren reappeared. Jerome was right behind them. Warren had a duffle bag.

"Thanks, Jerome," Paps said. "You were certainly an angel of mercy today."

"Anytime," Jerome said. He punched Warren's arm hard. "Good luck, kid. See you in the movies."

Warrior hugged Jerome. "Stay cool. Come see me some-time."

Paps opened the driver-side door. "I can drive to Amarillo, then you can take it from there," he said to Warrior. "Harlan, you get in the back for now."

I had to squeeze in the back? Well, fine, Grandfather and I would just sleep. I opened the back door. "Hand me the cooler," I said. "I'll find a spot for it back here."

Warrior opened the wagon door and handed me the cooler and his duffle bag, then sat down. He took a deep breath, then sniffed the air twice. "Peehew! Man, you got some serious B.O. in this car," he said. He turned to look at me. "What's in the box?"

"Bibles. Living Bibles," I said as I emptied the ice cooler.

"Kind of smells like *dead* Bibles," Warrior said. He chuckled to himself.

Paps cranked up the engine. "Well, boys, all set?" Paps asked. "Use your suitcase and the duffle bag to lean against, Harlan. That will make it almost comfortable."

I crammed the suitcase between the wheel well and Grandfather, then pushed the duffle bag against it and leaned back. The odor of formaldehyde did kind of hang around everywhere; but maybe with the air-conditioner on, it wouldn't be so noticeable. At least I didn't have to talk to Paps.

Paps turned out onto the highway. "Here we go again," he said. "We will stop for hamburgers or something the first chance we get. Cannot do the Lord's work on empty stomachs."

Mesquite trees and desert scrub zoomed past my window.

We pressed on beyond the two-lane highway, back onto the interstate. The land lay out wide and flat to the horizon, and a grain elevator stood lookout in the distance.

"This is going to work out just dandy," Paps said. "Why, we still might make it to the Cleavers' in time to watch *Campus Crusade for Christ* on TV."

Of course, up to now I had clean forgot about Connie Cleaver. For the next hundred miles, I looked just like that smiley face from Isa Faye's rhubarb pancakes. Was it a sin to be that happy?

CHAPTER

8

Warrior's soul was still up for grabs, although Paps worked hard at it all afternoon. To his credit, Warrior gave as good as he got—he must have read every one of those religious books at Jerome's. But we were still more than an hour away from the Cleavers', and Paps wasn't giving up. Not yet.

"Warren, if you do not have your own personal encounter with your Lord and Savior, you will be damned for eternity," Paps said. "You have got to accept salvation. There is no other way. There is no other hope. Jesus says, 'I am the way and the truth and the life.' It is right in the Bible, and the Bible is the undisputed word of the Lord."

Paps had handed off the driving to Warrior, who smiled like some Cheshire cat at all Paps's preaching.

"We're on the same side, Reverend," Warrior said. "I'm looking for a mystical experience—without a neat explanation of Heaven and Hell. How do we even know that Heaven and Hell are out there anyway?"

"It is in the Bible!"

"And that's it? Just because it's in the Bible you think Heaven and Hell are out there somewhere on the edge of the universe? Did you know that in the Middle East, man, they don't even think of Heaven and Hell as someplace outside the body?" Warrior tapped his chest. "It's all inside your heart and your head."

"Well, if they read the Bible they would know better," Paps said. "Without Jesus, damnation is all there is."

I bet Jesus didn't even make Warrior's top-ten list. Warrior had enlightened Paps with talk about Zen and his pal Buddha until Paps seemed about bumfuzzled at Warrior's religious leanings. To my way of thinking, he was making me look pretty good in Paps's eyes. I was beginning to like old Warrior.

Warrior looked over at Paps from the wheel. "I got a question for you, Reverend. Ever heard the sound of two hands clapping?"

"Sure," Paps said. He turned and looked back at me like I was supposed to know what Warrior was talking about. I had no idea.

"What's the sound of one hand clapping? Ever thought about that?" Warrior waited.

Paps frowned. "We, well, no, we . . ." Then Paps smiled in sudden recognition. "Why, one hand clapping would be no sound at all," he said.

"You're wrong, Reverend," Warrior said, turning back to look at the interstate. "It's not a trick question; you just can't imagine it."

No kidding.

"The Bible is just a lot of nice stories to me, man. Scripture forces your life energy into one way of thinking. Nothing personal, but I just don't relate."

"We would just hate to see you in Hell, Warren," Paps said.

"I'd hate for you to see me there, too, Reverend," Warrior said. He mugged his best Hollywood movie-star grin. " 'Cause that would mean we both fell a little short of our plans."

I held my hand over my mouth to keep from busting out laughing. Paps froze for a minute, then his mouth tittered sideways. It was one of the few times I'd seen Paps halfway smile. If Warrior could bring that out in Paps, what other miracles could he work?

"How did you get to be a preacher, Reverend?" Warrior asked. "Run in the family?"

"My father had nothing to do with the Good Book," Paps said. "Most likely, he lived a life of sin and degradation in Las Vegas. His soul is probably in Hell by now."

Warrior flipped his sunglasses to the top of his head. "So who are the Bibles for?"

Paps turned around on the edge of the front seat and gave me a "come to Jesus" look. "Harlan?" *Thou shalt not lie like a dog.*

"Bibles?" I tried to look innocent, but my voice cranked up an octave on the last syllable. That was a dead giveaway.

He turned back to Warrior. "Warren, we are afraid Harlan lied to you. There are no Bibles in that crate. Out of the blue, my father paid me a visit after twenty years, then promptly died of a heart attack. His will stipulated that his earthly remains had to be delivered to Las Vegas, but we could not afford to ship the body on an airplane, so we are driving the corpse to Las Vegas for burial."

"We? As in me? I'm driving a dead body to Las Vegas?" Warrior asked.

"That is a true statement," Paps said.

"In this station wagon? In that crate in the back of this station wagon?" Warrior glanced back at Grandfather and me.

"As the Lord is my shepherd," Paps said.

"Man, this is the weirdest thing I've ever heard. Are you putting me on?"

"He's been embalmed and all," I added. "I mean it's not like we're body snatchers or something. We've got the death certificate and everything. It's all official."

Warrior spoke slow, like he was trying to stay cool. "Okay, so we're driving your father's dead body back home to Las Vegas for the funeral?"

"Yes." Paps nodded his head.

"And he's in the crate in the back?" Warrior pointed to Grandfather.

"Yes. In the casket, in the crate," Paps offered up.

"Dead?"

"Why, yes, of course, yes," Paps said. "Already embalmed."

Grandfather was dead, in the crate, and we were headed for Las Vegas. Paps seemed so matter-of-fact about it, Warrior must have thought he was starring in an episode of *The Twilight Zone.*

"Grandfather's last request was to be buried in Las Vegas," I said. "We're taking his remains. . . ." My voice trailed off. I didn't want to go on explaining everything to Warrior.

I glanced at the crate next to me. Grandfather's body was probably a big old shriveled-up prune by now. But with all the talk, what about his soul? Was it in Hell like Paps said? Or just hitchhiking along to Las Vegas with us, like Warrior?

Warrior laughed. "Well, Reverend, this is a kick. Kind of like a flipped-out sitcom. You're not really vampires, are you?" Warrior laughed again.

Paps was dead serious. "We are sure this all seems a little unusual, Warren. But God is working through us, and we are just following His will.

"I guess truth is stranger than fiction," Warrior said. He glanced back at the crate one more time and settled back a little into the seat. "Okay, a lot stranger." Warrior drove for a minute without talking. "So your old man came back after twenty years? Did you get to talk to him?"

"No. Died of a heart attack before we even knew he was back in town," Paps said.

"And he wasn't a preacher?"

"Heavens, no," Paps answered. "My father did not care about the Lord."

"Why did your old man leave town in the first place?"

A big wide gulf of silence filled the car. I shifted forward to try and see Paps's reaction. I'd always been too terrified to ask why he and Grandfather had a parting of the ways. It's an old skeleton in our family closet, and nobody ever opened that door.

Paps looked straight ahead. "We do not talk about this much."

That was an understatement.

But Warrior didn't let Paps off the hook. "So why did your father leave?" The question hung in the air with the hum of tires rolling over the highway. Pap's jaw went tight.

"It is all water under the bridge. Things were always *complicated*." Paps paused for a moment. "My mother died a horrible death of breast cancer," he finally said.

A big old lump jumped up in the back of my throat. Paps hadn't said ten words about Grandmother in my whole life.

"The cancer was vicious and painful. Mother suffered something terrible. Harlan O argued with the doctors about how ineffective the cancer drugs were. How expensive they were. He blamed everybody, including God. He turned to the bottle, then to some friends he had made. People he hardly knew. People different from my mother."

"After the funeral, we suffered. We were lost." Paps's voice was tiny, pitiful even. "But in our despair, Jesus found us. On April 13, 1952, we met the Lord, and everything changed."

"You and your dad?" Warrior asked.

"Heavens no. My body and soul."

"Oh. So *you* were born again?" Warrior asked.

"God had called Mother back to Him and had saved us in the process. It was the Lord's plan for us both, and we begged Harlan O to accept it, but he refused. He cursed God. We argued. He left, and that was it."

I blinked hard. I hadn't known my grandparents one bit, but theirs sure was a sad story.

"That's pretty tough," Warrior said. "I'm sorry about your mom, Reverend. But how do you know your father didn't find salvation later?"

A sign said Albuquerque City Limits.

"My father was stubborn. He closed himself off from God."

"But you don't know for sure. 'Judge not lest ye be judged,' Reverend. The Bible says that."

"Well, it does not seem likely that he changed. He did end up in Las Vegas."

"Your old man could have come home to tell you he'd found God," Warrior said. "You don't know. Maybe your father's in Heaven with your mother right this very minute."

"We doubt it." Paps's voice seemed to break.

"You all right?" I asked, trying to be nice.

"We are tired, Harlan," Paps said. "It has been a long day."

Warrior didn't say anything else. He just drove.

I leaned back. I couldn't believe Paps spilled the beans about Grandfather and him to Warrior. An old feeling of sadness gripped me. Paps didn't get along with his daddy any better than I got along with Paps. It must be hereditary or something. I teared up some.

Before long, we pulled into the Cleavers' driveway. Connie and her little brother sat on the porch waiting for us. Connie had changed from a girl into a goddess. My spirits picked up, and I wiped my eyes. Some old feud between Paps and Grandfather didn't have nothing to do with me. Just seeing Connie made me forget all about it.

CHAPTER

9

"Sorry to hear about your father, Harlan P.," Mr. Cleaver said as he passed a lettuce salad around the table. "How's he holding up on the trip?"

I had just shoved a big forkful of Mrs. Cleaver's Spanish-rice casserole into my mouth, and I inhaled so hard, rice about went up my nose. Why didn't Paps just put an ad in the newspaper? Now everybody knew we were riding around with Grandfather in the back of the Chevy. I coughed up the rice and gulped down some iced tea.

"I appreciate your sympathy, Jimmy," Paps said. "It was a shock. But the Lord is working for us. We will have the remains in Las Vegas tomorrow, God willing."

"Amen," Mr. Cleaver said.

I ate some more rice and watched Connie. I couldn't take my eyes off her. But she couldn't take her eyes off Warrior, and he didn't look like he minded the attention too much. Connie's rich, flowing black hair, soft amber eyes, and come-on look made her seem older than sixteen. Of course, the fact that she now had a figure that didn't seem geometrically possible didn't hurt nothing.

I sopped a piece of white bread around my plate and tried not to think about the two lovebirds. Connie and Warrior could have been on another planet they were so wrapped up in each other. My heart ached just looking at them.

Seven-year-old Dusty stared at me from across the table. I pushed my plate to the side and tried to ignore him, but he was giving me the creeps. Dusty didn't look a thing like Connie; in fact, it was about impossible to believe he was even her brother. He was pale and wore a bow tie and worried a lot about germs.

"I bet you don't know President Nixon's middle name," he said.

"Sure I do," I said. "Milhous. Do you know he has a dog?" I wiped my chin with my napkin.

"Checkers!" Dusty said.

"Not anymore. Checkers is dead. Now he has an Irish setter or something. I saw it on television."

"It's Checkers," Dusty corrected me. "And I bet you don't even know where he was born."

"Old Tricky Dick was born in California," I said. Dusty's enthusiasm was about to get on my nerves.

"You called the president a bad name, and I'm going to tell."

"Fine with me," I said. "Who are you going to tell?" Dusty tried to kick my chair but missed. I ignored him and watched Warrior for a minute. Connie touched his tattoo and giggled. She never took her eyes off him. Not for a second. Of course, Mrs. Cleaver never took her eyes off Connie.

"Connie, why don't you help me with the dishes," Mrs. Cleaver said. She took their plates into the kitchen, and Connie followed. Connie gave Warrior a look that melted my socks. I couldn't have stood up at that moment if the house had been on fire.

I turned my attention back to Paps's conversation with Mr. Cleaver.

"I mentioned to Jennine about your opportunity for the radio outreach program," Mr. Cleaver told Paps. "I'm so happy to help you out on your mission for the Lord."

"We have had a discussion with the radio station manager in McKinney," Paps said. "We told him we would call him next week to discuss the details and look at a contract."

Warrior was listening now. "You're going to start a radio ministry?" he asked.

"That is the plan," Paps said. "If the Lord wills it. And so far the Lord is providing good people to help us. God is opening doors for us one right after another, right and left."

I squirmed and looked down at the tablecloth.

"Yeah, but a radio show takes some cash, man. I mean, *cha-ching*!" Warrior rubbed his thumb against his fingers. "You got that kind of change?"

"Well, not today, but we will on Monday," Paps said.

I frowned. I didn't think it was smart to tell Warrior and the rest of the world that we would be rich in a couple of days. People get strange about money, and we didn't know Warrior very well. Heck, we didn't even know the Cleavers, really. That kid Dusty could kill us all in our sleep and give the money to Nixon's reelection campaign in a heartbeat.

"My father left me fifty thousand dollars," Paps said. "We expect to receive the funds when we get to Las Vegas."

"I can just see you doing a radio show, man," Warrior said. He looked at me. "Harlan, are you in this deal, too?"

I didn't answer.

Mr. Cleaver patted the table. "Harlan P is living faith, I tell you. Do you know any other man who would take his daddy's dead body clean across the country to get money for a 'Praise the Lord' radio show?"

"Can't exactly say that I do," Warrior said.

This whole conversation was making me feel creepy. We weren't taking Grandfather to Las Vegas *just* to get a radio show.

"Dessert, anyone?" Mrs. Cleaver's head popped through the swinging door to the kitchen. "Chocolate mayonnaise cake coming right up!"

Chocolate and mayonnaise mixed up, baked, and slathered in icing tasted downright sinful. I ate two pieces of cake and about wanted to lick my plate but thought better of it. Of course, Dusty watched me the whole time. He sucked down his cake, then stomped and howled all the way upstairs when he was excused for bed. I was bushed myself and about ready to hit the sack, but I kept thinking about Grandfather out there in that box all alone.

"I think I'll just nap in the car tonight," I told Paps. "I don't feel right leaving Grandfather out there by himself."

"No, you go on to bed," Paps said. "We thought maybe we should go sit out there for a while." A gloominess had settled on Paps ever since he told Warrior about Grandfather's leaving, and even the cake hadn't stirred him out of it. I guess Paps did love Grandfather some.

"All right then. Good night."

But the good night didn't last long. At two in the morning, I heard a noise. Mrs. Cleaver had bunked Warrior and me in Dusty's room. Warrior and I flipped a quarter for the bottom bunk, and I won. Stripped down to my white briefs, I got into bed and was out like a light, but a noise woke me up.

For a minute, I didn't know where I was. The house was dead quiet. Warrior snored softly above me.

I turned over to face the wall and started to doze off again. But a light breath of air blew on the back of my neck. I felt a cold draft of air as the covers lifted and someone lay down next to me. I thought my heart would stop.

Silky legs rubbed along my thigh. Oh Lord, help me! I lay there, enjoying her lips on the back of my neck. It was so dark, neither one of us could see a thing, but my imagination was working pretty good. I rolled over and ran my hand down her back. She had on some sort of shorty pajamas and smelled like strawberries. Her hair was all tangled up over her face. I gently pushed back her hair, pulled her to me, and kissed her.

The lights went on. "What in the name of God?" Mrs. Cleaver yelled.

We sat up. Connie took one look at me, then screamed to high heaven. She slapped me hard across the face. She had a good right arm, too, and it hurt. Within seconds, the entire Cleaver family, including Dusty, stood at the door staring at me. Mrs. Cleaver held a trembling hand over her mouth and an arm around Connie. Connie was crying in her shorty pajamas. She looked beautiful. Mr. Cleaver stormed off to get Paps.

Warrior was awake by then, too. He leaned down from the top bunk. "Holy hell, Harlan," he said, yawning. Then he looked up at the Cleavers. "It's always the quiet guy—the one you never suspect."

About that time, Paps burst into the room carrying his Bible and pulled me to my feet. "Harlan Q, I ought to tan your hide," he said. "Is there nothing sacred to you? Their daughter? In their own home? You need to get down on your knees and beg the Almighty to forgive your sin and fornication."

Standing there in my white briefs and my puny white legs, I guess I looked kind of pathetic. Dusty giggled, and Connie started in a little too. It killed my soul to have Connie laughing at me like that. I felt lightheaded for a minute—almost nauseated. I snatched my blue jeans from the chair.

"God Almighty don't know nothing about this," I said. "To hell with you!" I yelled right into Paps's face. "To hell with all y'all!"

A hard slap came out of Paps's hand that about knocked me over. I sat back down on the bed. The side of my face burned, and a ringing ran through my ear to the top of my head.

"Whoa, Reverend!" Warrior jumped down from his bunk with his tanned, perfectly tight six-pack stomach. "I don't think you want to resort to violence here, man."

"Harlan Q tried to defile this young girl in her own home. She was saved only by a diligent mother and the grace of God." Paps talked fast, like he was sorry and nervous and angry all at once.

Warrior chuckled under his breath. "Reverend, you sure don't get out much."

My nose had started to bleed a little. I lifted my head and stared at the ceiling to keep the blood from running out my nose, rubbed the side of my face, and reached around to find a blanket to pull over me.

"Well, I think I know what was going on," Paps said.

"No, you don't!" I said. "*I* don't even know what was going on. Connie just came in here and jumped into bed."

We all looked at Connie. Her eyes darted to the floor. "I'll get a cold washcloth," she said.

"The devil's temptations are mighty," Paps said. "A boy has to be on guard. Diligent. Why, we never meant . . ." Paps's voice fell away in a murmur. "We never intended . . ."

I felt the blood trickle along my upper lip. For once Paps had to squirm in his own guilt, and it served him right.

"Don't bleed all over my blanket," Dusty yelled.

"Get back in bed," Mr. Cleaver said.

"If he gets blood all over my bed, I'm not going to sleep in there ever again."

"Go to bed!" Mr. Cleaver yelled. Dusty stormed down the hall but not without shouting back at the top of his lungs, "You'll be sorry if I get sick and die! Just wait and see!"

The overhead light glared at me. I had had about all I could stand of the whole Cleaver clan.

Connie came in with the washcloth, and Mr. Cleaver handed it to me. I pressed the cool cloth up against my face.

We all stared at Connie again. "What?" she said. "What?" Nobody answered. Her chin started quivering. Only just a hint at first.

"What were you doing in here?" Mrs. Cleaver asked. "I just assumed Harlan had somehow lured you into . . ."

Warrior interrupted, "No offense, but Harlan's just not her type, Mrs. Cleaver. I think she was looking for me, but I never asked her to come in here or anything else. She's underage." Warrior pulled a T-shirt over his head.

Connie's chin was a virtual earthquake now. Her face screwed up into a full-blown sob, and she tried to speak. With every word, more tears streamed down her face, and even I had to admit, the snot pouring from her nose made her a lot less pretty.

The more Connie tried to speak, the more she blubbered. Mrs. Cleaver gave her a sideways hug and a clean tissue.

The ceiling light cast a harsh glare over the room, so I leaned back under the shade of the bunk bed. I wondered if we all looked as old as I felt. Paps sat on a chair and studied the spine of his Bible, and Warrior stood with his Chinese tattoo running down his arm and his T-shirt tight across his perfect chest. I wiped the washcloth against my nose one last time.

"I'm waiting for an answer, young lady," Mr. Cleaver said.

Connie sniffed and blew her nose. "I don't remember," she said. "Maybe I was sleepwalking or something. One minute I was in my bedroom. I had a bad dream. Then, the next minute I was in here, and Mother turned on the light. I don't remember!"

I exchanged glances with Warrior.

"I was scared," Connie said. "I don't know what happened."

"Maybe if you were grounded for a month, your memory would get better," Mr. Cleaver said.

"No, Daddy! I wasn't . . . I didn't . . . I was so, so scared. In my dream, bad people were after me, and I was trying to find you and Mama." Connie whimpered into her tissue, then started bawling again. Connie's bold dishonesty made my little white lies seem innocent. That girl was a professional.

"Connie, are you okay? You seem so depressed lately," Mrs. Cleaver said. She hugged Connie to her.

Mr. Cleaver sighed. "Maybe we should all just get some sleep and sort this out in the morning," Mr. Cleaver said.

"I'm going to the bathroom," Warrior said.

Connie's crying settled into hiccups. Mrs. Cleaver patted her daughter's back. As Warrior slipped past them, the faintest smile crept across Connie's face. What an actress! Bitter pain jabbed into my shoulder. My exciting road trip to Las Vegas was feeling more like a train wreck. Why couldn't I ever get the beautiful girl?

"I guess y'all want to head out early," Mr. Cleaver said. From the edge in his voice, it wasn't a question.

"I think we should," Paps said. "We will be gone by seven."

"Connie's a healthy girl. That's been a challenge lately," Mr. Cleaver said. "Just pray for her, will you, Reverend?" He shook Paps's hand. "Good night," he said. "Mrs. Cleaver will spend the night in Connie's room. She won't bother you boys anymore."

I laid the washcloth on the nightstand and pulled the sheet and blanket around me. I didn't even take off my jeans.

Paps spoke. "We acted before we thought," he said. "And that was wrong. We shall ask the Lord's forgiveness. But, Harlan, a man cannot give in to the temptations of the flesh. Pray for God to deliver you from evil, son. Pray hard for his forgiveness." His voice was flat and tired.

If God didn't know there was nothing to forgive, I sure wasn't going to tell him. "Yeah, I'll do that," I said.

Paps nodded and stood up. "We will wake you about five so we can get on the road. Tell Warren, if you don't mind."

I didn't answer. I turned to the wall and buried myself in the covers.

Paps stood there for a moment, then his footsteps echoed down the hall and out the front door.

Warrior clicked off the light and bounded up into the top bunk. "You got to let your anger go, Harlan." Warrior's voice came out of the dark. "You've got to free yourself from hate, man—and from love, too, for that matter. If you don't, they'll end up owning you."

"What are you talking about?" I asked.

"Buddha said to want for nothing; only then can you find everything."

"Go to sleep," I said. I pulled the blanket tighter around me. Warrior was as crazy as Paps. My eyes watered, and I clenched them tight.

I shoved my pillow against my neck and stared into the night. Tears slid down my face into the inside of my ears. We would be in Las Vegas tomorrow night. All I needed was to see Grandfather buried, and then I could get the hell away from Paps.

And not just across town to the Hamiltons. Far away. Up East, maybe. Or Mexico. My grandfather didn't have dibs on running away.

CHAPTER
10

The next morning, we left the Cleavers' house and headed west on Interstate 40 to Arizona. The countryside opened up and the sky was as tall as Heaven against the rugged desert.

"Doing okay?" Paps turned around and gave me a weak smile like we were all hunky-dory.

"Fine," I said.

"Need anything?"

"No."

"Hungry?"

"No."

I'd been plotting all morning how I might take off for good. This time I had to be cool and collected—not hopping mad like the time I ran off to the Hamiltons. I figured the only way I could really run away forever was with some money, and I didn't have twenty dollars to my name. Grandfather's fifty thousand dollars would do the trick, but the only way I could get it was to steal it, and I didn't want to turn criminal just yet.

Paps turned his attention to Warrior. "What are your plans once we get into Las Vegas, Warren?" he asked.

"Find a flophouse for a couple of days and get a job," Warrior said. "I can't work at the casinos because I'm only nineteen, but I'll find something. I'm pretty handy with tools. Maybe work construction. Work for a few weeks, then head to L.A."

"You said you were from Dallas?" Paps asked.

"Big D it is," Warrior said. "But I want to be an actor, and you got to be in L.A. or New York for that. I've been California dreaming since I was Harlan's age."

"That is a hard life, acting for a living," Paps said.

"Different hard," Warrior said. "It's tough to get a break, but I'm young. Pretty good face. Decent body. And I can memorize just about anything. Sometimes, I can memorize lines by reading them just once. That about drove my high school drama teacher nuts."

"Photographic memory? Well, goodness gracious," Paps said.

I butted in. "You mean you can remember anything you see?"

"Almost," Warrior said. "When I was three, my father would stand me up in the middle of the dining-room table so I could recite Bible verses after Sunday lunch." Warrior shrugged. "It was kind of weird. That's probably why I don't read the Bible now, but I bet I'm about the only nineteen-year-old alive who knows the whole New Testament by heart."

"You do?" I asked. The only part I knew was the Christmas story from Luke and that was only because I wanted to be one of the Wise Men in the third-grade Christmas pageant so I could wear my bathrobe to Sunday church.

"Just ask me," Warrior said. "Go ahead."

Paps glanced over at Warrior. "Pick a hard one, Harlan Q. Perhaps we can trip him up." Paps grinned.

I sighed. "Hold on," I said. "Hold on. Let me think." The engine of the station wagon whined along the asphalt. "John, chapter 20, verse 32."

"There is no verse 32, Harlan," Paps said with a disappointed glance.

"Well, why don't you ask then?"

Paps didn't say anything; he just handed his Bible back over the seat to me. I flipped through the pages. "How about John, chapter 20, verse 29."

Warrior closed his eyes for a few seconds. "'Jesus saith unto him, Thomas, because thou hast seen me, thou hast believed: blessed are they that have seen, and have believed.'"

"That's pretty close," I said. "The last few words are mixed up."

"Give me another," Warrior said.

I thumbed forward a few pages. "Acts, chapter 19, verse 11."

"'And God wrought special miracles by the hands of Paul.'" Warrior smiled without opening his eyes.

"Right on," I said. "But that was an easy one."

"Go on," Warrior said. "Make it harder."

Again, I flipped forward. "Second Corinthians, chapter 1, verse 4."

"'Who comforteth us in all our tribulation, that we may be able to comfort them which are in any trouble, by the comfort wherewith we ourselves are comforted of God.'"

I let out a low whistle. "Perfect," I said. Warrior turned back in his seat and bowed to the dashboard.

"That is amazing," Paps said. "You have a gift from the Heavenly Father, Warren. I hope you do not waste it on acting."

"I don't consider acting a waste," Warrior said. "Pardon me, Reverend, but I'm good with my life, man."

It was plumb remarkable the way Warrior talked to Paps. Real polite like and all, but he cut right to the chase. Paps didn't have a chance to preach.

Paps kept his eyes on the highway and his jaw popped. I couldn't tell what he was thinking. "What moved you away from God, Warren? It is a long road from the dining-room table to Los Angeles," Paps said.

"I wanted to decide on my own about God and faith, but my father wouldn't let me," Warrior said. "It was his way or the highway. And when he put it like that, the highway looked pretty good."

I waited for Paps to start up. About a million billboards and trailer parks went by. Paps flicked his thumb against his ear. Over and over and over. Eternity passed.

Finally, Paps spoke. "Warren, do you love your father?" he asked.

"Yes, I do," Warrior said. "But it's not about love or hate, man. It's about acceptance. I try to accept him as he is and hope he can do the same for me someday."

Paps glanced over at Warrior. "You are wrong, Warren. It is very much about love. If your father accepts you as you are, you will be lost forever. Your soul will be damned for eternity. He cannot give up on you. Not if he really loves you."

Warrior leaned over to Paps. "Maybe my dad would do a lot better to just love me unconditionally." Warrior's voice was real low, and I had to lean forward to hear him. "You know, you can't bully someone into believing, Reverend."

It might as well have been the tribulation. I sucked air into my lungs hard. Paps wasn't going to let Warrior talk to him like that. He would just pull the car over and tell Warrior to get out, thank you very much.

But Paps drove on in silence for a full five minutes. "Well, do not give up on God," he said finally. "Or on your father, either." Paps glanced back in the rear-view mirror and stared at me.

What was he looking at? I stared back. Paps looked away.

Warrior put on his sunglasses and leaned against the passenger window. Within about two minutes, he was dead to the world asleep. Maybe me and Warrior had more in common than I realized. *Thou shalt doubt the faith of thy fathers.*

And that's when it struck me. Sure, he talked about being some L.A. actor, but when it came right down to it, Warrior was running away, too. Maybe he needed some company. Maybe that company could be me.

11

Paps drove straight into the morning. It was time for lunch before we stopped. "Harlan, are you awake?" Paps was all gung ho and cheerful.

"Wide awake and starving," I said, stretching against the duffel bag. I looked around for a minute. "Where are we?"

"Winslow, Arizona," Paps said. "Thought you boys might be hungry." He turned off the car engine. "We will get some gasoline, then we can eat."

"Is that little angel in your pocket going to pump the gas?" I asked.

Paps flipped open the glove compartment and pulled out a tire gauge. "How many times do *I* have to apologize?" Paps asked. "Is it possible that *you* might forgive last night?"

I stared out the window.

Paps shook Warrior on the arm. "Warren, it is time for lunch, son."

Warrior stirred and opened his car door. "Oh, man, we're on Route 66," he said. "That's cool."

"It is all God's journey," Paps said. He waved the tire gauge and turned to the station attendant.

Warrior yawned and climbed out of the car. "What we need is a convertible, Reverend. I bet old Gramps here would get a kick out of riding down Route 66 in the back of a convertible."

Paps didn't answer. I imagined me and Grandfather in his chromed-up Eldorado with the wind in our hair. It would have been great.

Warrior stretched his arms out into the sky, then slapped the top of the station wagon and opened my car door. He put out his hand and heaved me from the car in one swift motion, like I was a five-pound barbell. His Warrior tattoo rippled across his arm. I steadied myself on the car door.

The restaurant was actually in an old stone building next door to the gas station. A huge circle of a plate-glass window that was taller than me faced the street. The sign above it read Moon Wok Cafe.

Paps came around the car, organizing his folding money. "I hope you boys like Chinese food," he said. "There is just so much to celebrate on this God-given day. Praise the Lord."

Warrior and I exchanged glances. Paps should just give it a rest.

Inside, the restaurant was small, with Formica-chipped tables and plastic-covered booths lining the walls. The restaurant wasn't busy; in fact, we were pretty much the only people in there, except for a couple of state troopers drinking coffee. The waitress brought us menus, water, and silverware, wrapped in paper napkins.

"Any recommendations?" Paps asked.

"How would I know?" I asked. I studied the menu. Isa Faye had once made stir-fried beef with a bunch of peppers and onions. That seemed safe.

"Warren, let us pay for your meal," Paps said. "What will you have?" Paps's voice had an upbeat tone.

Warrior perused the menu and drank his water. "Pretty much the whole left side of the page," he said. Warrior's joke was about as old as the hills, but I smiled. Paps nodded and gave me a kind of wink, like we shared some big secret.

The waitress came to take our order. She was Asian, about four feet tall, and chunky, like a kid's building block.

"Harlan Q?" Paps said.

"Stir-fried beef," I said, "with sweet tea."

"The same," Paps added.

The waitress took a long time writing down our order on a little pad of paper. She looked up at Warrior. "I know already what you want," she said. She grinned about as wide as a four-lane highway. "Moo goo gai pan!"

Warrior looked confused. "No moo goo gai pan, but thanks, anyway."

"No?" she said. "You don't want moo goo gai pan?" She seemed a little disappointed. She raised her eyebrows.

"No," Warrior said. "Sweet-and-sour pork. One order of sweet-and-sour pork, with a Coke."

The woman breathed a shy giggle. "But tattoo . . . " The waitress's teeth overlapped, and her nails were bitten down to the quick, but I couldn't help but like her.

"You read Chinese?" Warrior interrupted. He pointed to his arm. "It says *Warrior.* This Chinese guy—a friend of mine in Dallas—wrote it out when I got my tattoo. Pretty cool, huh?"

Then the girl broke out in a full-fledged giggle fit. "Tattoo . . . tatt . . . taa . . ." She couldn't even say the word for laughing. She shifted her weight from one foot to the other. "But tattoo . . ." She broke into breathy giggles again.

"What?" I said. "What?"

"Miss, what is so funny?" Paps sounded irritated.

"Moo goo gai pan," she finally managed to say. She took a deep breath and blew some air out across the table. "Friend make mistake. Your tattoo say *moo goo gai pan*."

"What?" Warrior said.

"Moo goo gai pan," the hostess said. "Your friend funny."

Warrior blinked real hard a couple of times. The waitress grinned and nodded at Paps, but he didn't react. She nodded again and smiled warmly at Warrior. "No be sad," she said. "Moo goo gai pan veeery goood." She walked back into the kitchen.

Warrior looked at his arm. The Chinese writing snaked down his bicep. He looked up at Paps and then at me. And then at Paps again.

"Well, you can always be a warrior for Christ, Warren," Paps said.

I gave Paps a "shut-up" look.

Warrior gave us both a stupid grin. "Moo goo gai pan?" he asked. "Moo goo gai pan? So now I'm the moo goo gai pan man?"

I laughed at Warrior's joke. Old Warrior.

Warrior laughed, too. "It's cool," he said. "I'm cool with it. I'm cool. Definitely cool."

"Hey, Moo Goo," I said.

"Call me Moo," Warrior said. "But don't be telling me I'm full of bull." He pointed his finger at me and about knocked over my water. I caught the glass just before it dumped into Paps's lap. I couldn't stop myself from laughing some more, and I kind of felt better.

"Boys, I think it is time to behave," Paps said. "We are in a public place."

About that time, the waitress brought us our food. She put the plates on the table. "Old Chinese proverb say " 'A smile gain you ten more years of life,' " she said. "Friend give gift."

Warrior nodded his head. "I guess I'll have to go with that," he said. "Maybe I can tell people that moo goo gai pan is some far-out guru or something. That sounds kind of cool."

The waitress just nodded some more. "Enjoy," she said.

"Dear Lord, thank you for this food we are about to receive," Paps said. "Amen."

I shoved a bite of stir-fried beef in my mouth with no amens about it and ate until I was about sick.

The waitress brought the check and some fortune cookies. "Good for digestion. Maybe for luck, too!" she said.

Paps got up and went to pay the check.

"What does yours say?" I asked Warrior as we followed Paps out to the car.

" 'Never trust friends who claim to know a foreign language.' "

I smiled.

"I'm just kidding. It says 'You're an old soul.' "

"What does that mean?" I asked.

"It means that I am wise," Warrior said.

"So you're a wise guy?" I asked.

"How 'bout yours?"

"'You will lose everything but find it again,'" I said.

"That's kind of deep," Warrior said.

"My grandfather died, and that was a loss."

"Well, I hope *he's* not coming back."

Paps unlocked the car. "Those fortune cookies are nothing but silliness. Only the Lord knows our future."

"You're probably right about that, Reverend," Warrior piped up. "The problem is to figure out who the Lord is in the first place."

Paps couldn't resist the bait, and he and Warrior started off on another argument of the faithful. Warrior was a godsend.

CHAPTER

12

"So, you mean to tell me that the Hopi Indians believe everything in nature has a soul? Even a rock?" Paps said. "Why, that is blasphemous."

Warrior and Paps had traded driving and were full into their little discussion on God, only this time Warrior had Paps on the defensive, explaining endless details about Native American Indian gods and spirits. I was sick to death of religion—period, no matter whose god it was.

"Not a soul, Reverend. A spirit," Warrior said. "The word is *kachina*—ancient ancestors who act on our behalf. Kind of like good angels."

Paps flipped the pages of his Bible like he was looking for some special passage.

Warrior pressed on. "Kachinas listen to people's prayers, then pass those prayers along to the gods. It's this whole organic cycle, man—nature, people, spirit, and the universe. It's really Zen."

"It is a universe of hogwash," Paps said. "Religion has nothing to do with nature. It is between God and man."

I resented every little saved hair on the back of Paps's perfectly combed head.

"Here it is," Paps said with a start, "right here in the Sermon on the Mount. When it comes to the birds in the air, Jesus says, 'Are you not much more valuable than they?' See, that passage proves that only human beings have souls. Birds and plants and rocks are temporary. Only people are eternal."

"Reverend, the Hopi are ancient people, man," Warrior said "They've lived around here for a thousand years. I don't think they are into much of the Bible."

"Well, they should be. It is ridiculous for people to expect salvation for a rock. A rock is not a living thing. It cannot have a soul. It cannot tremble at the sight of the Lord. It cannot fear eternal Hell and cannot look forward to paradise with our Lord."

"Depends on how you look at it, I guess," Warrior said. "Buddha says that nothing is lost in the universe. You know, lots of people in the world don't exactly agree with the Bible."

Paps looked kind of addled, like it had never occurred to him that someone would actually snub the Bible. "What do you think, Harlan?" Paps turned around and leaned against the driver's side door. "Do you think Warren is right?"

"About rocks?" I asked.

"About rocks having spirits," Paps said. "Rocks receiving salvation from the Almighty Lord." Paps looked eager for me to answer. He waited, listening.

"How would I know? Don't drag me into it."

"Well, you have read the Bible," Paps said. "And we both know you have opinions." A half-crooked smile came upon his face. This was his twisted way of getting on my good side.

"I don't know."

"I doubt that."

"I don't know. I don't care."

"But, you have to care, Harlan. God wants you to care."

"I just wish we could have about five minutes in this car without talking about God," I said. "Who cares if rocks have souls? Let them. It's fine with me."

Paps stopped smiling. "Do not be disrespectful. It was just a simple question. We just asked."

"I swear to Buddha, you and Warrior are about driving me batty," I said. A wobbly breath escaped from my lungs. "Could we just talk about the weather or something else like normal people?"

"Easy, man," Warrior said. "Don't get so uptight." He adjusted the rear-view mirror and our eyes met. "I'm just searching, you know? Trying to find my path."

"To what?" I said.

"I'm not as lucky as the Reverend here. I'm still looking for the meaning of life, I guess. I need to know if there's a point to all this. That maybe we do end up in some kind of paradise after all."

"Fat chance," I said. My throat choked up, small and unforgiving.

Paps's eyes turned dark, and his voice came out hard. "Harlan, you need to watch yourself. God does not want your blasphemy," he said. I guess he was done trying to make up.

"Let him talk, man," Warrior said.

I sucked air into my chest as far as I could, but a crushing weight stopped me short. A miserable sob came up from the back of my throat, and I tried to shut it down, but it got the best of me. My voice was all hoarse and shaky, but words fumed out of my mouth. Nothing could stop them.

"My blasphemy? What about you? What about your blasphemy? All you do is scream and shout that God's got us all damned. You go around scaring the bejesus out of people and calling that religion."

My eyes watered up with tears. "When I was a little kid, I was so terrified of God, I used to lie in bed at night waiting for Him to show up and damn me for chewing gum in social studies. I was scared stiff with all your harping about Hell."

My voice broke down to a breathless whisper. "You preach nothing but fear and judgment. Not even a rock would want salvation like that."

Paps's face flashed the enthusiasm of a preacher. "God should be feared, sir, with everything in your mind, your heart, and your soul! One day He will judge you for all eternity, and you have plenty to fear, young man."

"Why don't you just give it a break?" I whispered. I tried to catch my breath, but my throat was caught in a chokehold that wouldn't let go.

"Fear is just one step from salvation, Harlan Q! And we want your soul in Heaven, son!"

I gasped for air, panicked, and breathed faster, but no air came. A loud, raw wheezing sound came out of my lungs.

Paps clutched his Bible to him and started to pray. "Lord, God of Heaven and Earth, heal this boy. Take his fear and doubt, and save his soul."

"Stt . . . stt . . . stop!" I cried. "Stop!" Invisible hands clamped on my throat and crushed out every single speck of oxygen. No air to breathe. Tears squeezed out of my eyes. My lungs wheezed again.

Paps turned around, leaned over the seat, and grabbed my collar. A demon energy came out of his eyes. "Pray with me, Harlan! Pray with me!"

I blinked hard, gasped, and sputtered. The wheezing sound came again, bitter and uncontrollable. I swapped looks with Warrior as he glanced back to change lanes. "Hold on, man," he said. He swerved over to the next exit.

"Harlan, feel God's presence right here and now!" Paps yelled. "Heal this boy, Lord! Let his soul be surrounded by the power of your Almighty love!"

The wheezing roared louder. I tried to breathe, but I couldn't. No air. Lightheaded. Suffocating. Warrior slammed on the brakes, and Paps about flew into the windshield, but he grabbed tighter to my shirt and nearly pulled me over the front seat to him.

His face screamed into mine. "Save him now, Lord! Save him now!"

Before I knew it, Warrior had opened the back door and jerked me away from Paps and around toward him, so my feet were on the ground.

"Get your head down between your knees," he said. "Man, you're going to pass out right here."

I coughed up air. Warrior bent my head down toward the pavement. "You're hyperventilating, man. You got to relax.

Try to calm down. Breathe. Breathe slow." Warrior held his hand on the back of my neck to keep my head even with my knees.

For a minute, I was ready to faint dead away. My head was like a merry-go-round. Everything went kind of fuzzy, and the lights were getting dimmer—but it was broad daylight. I thought I might fall right over onto the spinning concrete. I leaned forward and closed my eyes. Then, in a heartbeat, it all stopped.

For no reason, something relaxed in my chest. The grip on my lungs was gone, and I felt my throat open up normal. I coughed and wiped my nose on my hand. My breathing came deep and slow, and my fuzzy brain cleared out. The concrete didn't move anymore, but tears flowed out of my eyes and down my face, and I was bawling hard.

Warrior bent down to me. "You okay, buddy?" he asked. He had to have seen my tears, but he didn't say anything. I cried like a kid right there up close in front of him for what must have been ten minutes or even more. Finally, I ran my hand over my eyes and tried to hush up.

"Amen, hallelujah," Paps said. "God is working on you, Harlan!" Paps paced up and down the pavement, holding his Bible. "Why, there is not a rock in this whole desert that God wants more than you, Harlan. We feel Him working on you, son. Zeroing right in on you. God is not going to let you get away. I know it."

I clenched my teeth tight to keep the tears inside. My breathing settled some. A stinging shame rolled right over me.

Warrior had seen me acting like a sniveling scaredy-cat kid.

Paps stopped in front of me and knelt down. "You just got to let go and receive the Lord into your heart, son. You cannot be worried about this life. Think about the rest of eternity, Harlan. That is what we want for you."

A truck sped by the outside lane. A sweltering breeze from the open door caught the side of my face. I wiped my eyes again.

"Fear the Lord, Harlan," Paps said, "and you are one step closer to Heaven."

At that moment, I hated Paps. And God, too, for that matter. I rubbed my hand over my hair and tried to mash my cowlick into my skull. I prayed Warrior wasn't there staring at me the whole time. A low-pitched nausea lingered in my stomach. I leaned down and breathed a good deep breath of air and caught a whiff of Grandfather in my lungs.

Paps patted my knee and stood up. I guess he figured the Lord was done with me for now. "Warren, take a break, and I will drive now," Paps said. He took the keys and walked around to the driver's side, his energy pumping.

Warrior waited. A hot blast of air from a passing car surrounded us. Then, the breeze died, and it was still. Hot and still. "They say God is love," Warrior said quietly. "You just got to go with that, man. Your anger will kill you." Pity hinged in his words. It was hard to take Warrior feeling sorry for me like that.

"Yeah. Praise the Lord. Hallelujah," I said. Warrior didn't let on if he heard the mocking pitch of my voice. I pulled my feet back into the station wagon and shut the door. He slid into the passenger side.

Paps reached back and patted the back of the seat. Then he smiled and pulled out onto the interstate. Warrior clicked on a radio station out of Flagstaff. Nobody talked.

Inside I felt like a semitrailer truck had just run over me. I slipped down, leaned my head on Grandfather's crate, and looked out the window. Some old Elvis song played on the radio.

I had to get Grandfather taken care of in Las Vegas, somehow convince Warrior that he had to help me, then find some money. Even if it meant stealing it and living a life of crime. I couldn't stomach Paps any more. And I wasn't going to.

CHAPTER
13

For the next two hours, not one single syllable was said about salvation. Or anything else. Paps flicked his ear, and Warrior fiddled around trying to find a clear radio signal. The only talk came from the radio—a cheery voice singing "You deserve a break today" and some chatty news announcer joking about a two-bit break-in someplace in Washington, D.C. I just looked out the window.

Soon, the scenery of scrub and rolling desert hills vanished into skinny pine trees and jagged earth where the highway was cut through the mountains. The station wagon's engine barreled up the incline, and the radio finally gave way to nothing but static. Warrior clicked it off.

I closed my eyes. My hyperventilating fit had about zapped my energy, so I must have drifted off to sleep until my own snoring woke me up. A highway sign announced the Nevada state line.

"Welcome to Nevada," Paps said. The sun eased long shadows over the countryside. "Almost there, God willing!"

Warrior leaned back over the seat like I was the poster child for terrorized preachers' kids or something. "Hey, Harlan, you okay?"

"How was that nap, son? Can you feel the Lord working

on you?" Paps looked back at me with eager enthusiasm, but I didn't answer.

"We need to call Mr. Stiletto for directions to the funeral home soon as we get into town," Paps continued. "Should be there in an hour or so."

An hour. That got me going a little. In an hour we would actually be in Las Vegas. I yawned again, adjusted the duffel bag, and sat up.

"Maybe we can meet with Mr. Stiletto tomorrow even though it is Sunday," Paps said. "Maybe right after the service?" Paps was a regular Chatty Cathy now. "Then we can head home on Monday morning. That would be good. We could meet with the radio station people by the end of the week. How does that sound, Harlan Q?"

"Sure," I said, hoping that I would be missing in action by then. "That's great, Paps."

"Oh yeah, man, I meant to ask you about the radio show," Warrior said. "What are you planning, Reverend?"

"To witness and save souls," Paps said. "That is the Lord's plan. But we can also envision a sermon and prayer requests, perhaps."

"So people can call in?" Warrior asked.

"Uh, well, we are not sure just yet how it all might work," Paps said. "But that is the plan."

Warrior turned around to talk to me. "One time when I was about eleven, I phoned into the *Call for Christ* prayer line and sang the song 'Jeepers Creepers' right on the air," Warrior said.

"You did?" I asked. That was about as bad as my Jesus list; old Warrior wasn't so much different from me.

"Man, my dad kicked my butt all the way to Fort Worth over that one. I cried like a baby."

"Why did you do it?" I asked. "Was it a bet or something?"

Warrior shrugged. "I was just a kid. It seemed funny. No big evil motive or anything."

"Did it occur to you that it might be seen as disrespectful?" Paps asked. He didn't seem to think it was so funny.

"Sure," Warrior said. "But I was just a kid. Kids do dumb things. I did worse."

"Like what?" I leaned forward and rested my chin on the back of the car seat.

"Did drugs for most of middle school. Ran away. Almost got married when I was seventeen. A real babe, too. About broke my heart."

"Holy smokes," I said. My raising was a cakewalk compared with Warrior's.

"But it was all dumb stuff," Warrior said. "Everything worked out okay."

"You must have taken your father on quite a ride," Paps said. "Hard to imagine . . ."

"We had our trials and tribulations, Reverend, that's for sure." Warrior grinned. "But we just kept on truckin'. Kind of like you and Harlan here."

"You said you loved your father, Warren," Paps said. "Do you ever talk to him?"

"Let's just say we're taking a time-out right now."

"You should call him," Paps said. "The Commandments tell us to honor thy father." Paps glanced back at me.

Warrior just shook his head and laughed. "I *am* honoring him, Reverend," he said. "Hey, I'm a good guy. I'm honest. I work hard. And I'm searching to find some kind of peace for myself in the world. What else could my dad want?" Warrior shrugged. "What else could any father want?"

That shut Paps up; he didn't even try to argue or debate with Warrior at all. Warren Ducklo was my hero about then.

We curved around the top of a cliff, and Hoover Dam lay out before us bigger than downtown Dallas. It was one huge slab of concrete, and the whole station wagon was like one of the little black ants that hung around the back porch door at the Hamilton-Johnston.

We drove down the curving two-lane to the bottom of the dam and back up the other side. The whole place was full of rocks and walls of thick cement, holding back a huge lake of water that lingered out over the horizon. The afternoon sun shimmered on the waves.

"We cannot stop," Paps warned before I even asked. "We need to be in town by six."

The station wagon chugged along in the desert heat. We drove the last ten miles into Las Vegas in the quiet, with Grandfather lingering in the air. He had made it home.

Up ahead, huge casinos and hotels just grew up out of the sand. Signs hawked loose quarter-slot machines, lucky dice, and winning tables. A couple of low mountains skirted the far horizon. Las Vegas looked a little cheap but alive. Fancy cars darted in and out of traffic. People were everywhere. Lights winked at us from every corner. It was Heaven.

Paps was taking in the sights, too. His back stiffened in the driver's seat, and he scowled at almost every new intersection of pretty girls and blinking lights. It was clear he didn't find Las Vegas so wonderful.

Finally, Paps pulled over at a combination liquor store, bait shop, and bingo hall. "Guess we better stop and call Mr. Stiletto," he said. There was a phone booth on the side of the building. "You boys stay here. Lock the doors and be careful. We will be right back." Paps hugged his Bible to his chest, got out of the car, and walked around the building.

Careful? Like someone would want to mess with a couple of teenagers and a corpse? The thrill of actually being in Las Vegas grabbed hold of me like a full-grown rattlesnake. I pounded on Grandfather's crate. "Harlan O! You're home!" I could see him smiling.

Warrior just shook his head. There we were, two PKs and a runaway grandfather, sitting pretty in Las Vegas. I smiled at Warrior and started to ask if I could crash with him for a while, but Paps came back and we headed straight to the funeral home. My asking would have to wait.

CHAPTER

14

Mr. Stiletto met us at Crook & Sons Funeral Home and Crematory and helped unload Grandfather onto a gurney. The prep room was cold stainless steel and Formica. I couldn't imagine much comfort coming from Crook or his sons. They were no Mr. Hamilton.

Stiletto was a big disappointment, too. He couldn't have been three inches taller than me with smooth brown hair and a baby-face smile that resembled one of those mannequins in a department store. He didn't look one bit scary. Besides, a Corleone would never dress like that. Stiletto wore a lime green, western-cut cowboy suit with matching cowboy boots. Nobody wore suits like that, except maybe Glen Campbell or Porter Waggoner.

When Paps introduced us, Stiletto pumped my hand with a powerful shake that made me wince. "Here's my card, kiddo," he said as he handed me a smooth white rectangle. "So you're Harlan Q?" The man never let me answer. "I bet you take after your mother's side of the family. Now, your old man here is the spitting image of your grandfather. By God, the spitting image."

Your old man was Paps. Paps frowned. "Mr. Stiletto and I have a little business here, Harlan Q. Perhaps you could get the paperwork out of the station wagon."

"It was a pleasure." Mr. Stiletto pumped my hand again. "Your grandfather was a good old boy. Jesus holy hell, we'll miss him."

Paps flinched at the Lord's name taken in vain but eased Mr. Stiletto down the sidewalk out of earshot. I wanted to stay around and listen to the conversation, but Paps wasn't about to include me in anything.

Warrior and I walked back to the car to get the death certificate. It didn't seem like a good time to get into a conversation with Warrior about running away just yet.

"Doesn't that guy Stiletto look like a slick Wayne Newton to you?" Warrior asked.

"I don't even know who Wayne Newton is."

"He guest-starred on *The Tonight Show* a few months ago. He's a singer. I think he even lives here in Las Vegas."

"Never seen him," I said. "Stiletto is my grandfather's attorney. He gave me his card." I pulled the card out of my pocket and handed it to Warrior.

"Hey, man, he's a gambler, too. I've never seen that combination before."

"What?"

"Says right here on his card. *Professional gambler.*"

I grabbed the card from Warrior's hand. The words were printed in raised gold letters right below his name: *Attorney-at-Law, Professional Gambler.*

"Can he do that?" I asked. "Be both?"

"Gambling is legal in Nevada, so why not?"

Stiletto seemed too flashy to be in the Mob, but maybe it

wasn't impossible. This was Las Vegas, wasn't it, and what good was Las Vegas without a few shady lawyers and double-dealers? I had a new respect for Mr. Stiletto. I stuffed the card in my back pocket.

"Here's the envelope from the funeral home in Bean's Creek," I said when we walked back from the car.

One of the Crook sons opened the flap but never changed expressions. "Everything looks in order," he said. He didn't seem at all sad for Paps or me. I could never imagine crying on that guy's shoulder. I missed the Hamiltons; Grandfather deserved a little genuine grief.

Mr. Stiletto handed the Crook boys a fat white envelope with what looked like cash stuffed in it. "The funeral will be at one tomorrow afternoon at the Hopewell Chapel Fellowship of Faith," he said. "You got directions? Be there early. I imagine there'll be a large crowd—may be a little rowdy, too."

"A crowd?" Paps asked.

"Your father was a popular barkeep," Mr. Stiletto said. "He gave comfort to a lot of people, you know what I mean? I'm sure they'll want to return the favor."

"What *do* you mean?" Paps asked.

I inched closer to hear. Grandfather was a bartender?

"Your father was part owner of a local bar—Long Gone Daddy's. Over on East Charleston, not far from downtown. Popular hangout. Big crowd there every night, even on Sundays— a lot of the patrons will probably show up for the service."

I saw Pap's spine go rigid. "My father was friends with a bunch of alcoholics?"

Mr. Stiletto smiled a sideways kind of smirk. "It was business," he said. "Drink a little. Talk a little. Drink a little. People get friendly. You know what I mean?" He held out his hand to Paps. "See you in the morning. All the arrangements are complete. I have a map if you didn't get directions."

He nodded and one of the Crooks took a map from his pocket and handed it to me.

"Thank you," I said. "Could I borrow your phone?"

Paps looked over at me.

"Just wanted Mr. Hamilton to know Grandfather got here in one piece." But I really just wanted to hear Mr. Hamilton's voice.

"Oh, of course," Paps said. "We do need to let the funeral director in Bean's Creek know we got here. My son will call collect if we can use your phone."

One of the Crooks nodded. "There's a phone just inside my office. I'll show you."

"Hurry it along, Harlan," Paps said. "We need to get going."

I followed the man into an office. "Dial nine to get an outside line," he said. "Don't worry about calling collect." The man's voice was deadpan. "We'll just add it to your bill."

I dialed the number and waited. My heart about skipped a beat when Isa Faye answered the phone before it even rang.

"Hello?"

"Hello! Hello! Isa Faye?"

"Harlan, is that you all the way from Las Vegas? Why, the phone didn't even ring! I picked it up to call down to the hospital."

"It's me," I said. "Direct from the Las Vegas Strip. I called to tell Mr. Hamilton that we got Grandfather delivered safe and sound. Not a scratch on the crate."

"Oh," Ida Faye said. "Mr. Hamilton's on a call out to the nursing home. I know he'll be sorry he missed talking to you, Harlan. How's everything going?"

"No complaints. I'm finding out things about Grandfather. He owned a bar and had lots of friends. Didn't have one thing to do with the Mob."

"Well, I'll be. How's your daddy holding up?"

"Just the same, nothing ever changes with him."

"Try to hang on now, honey. Take care best you can. I know it means a lot to him just to have you there."

"Yeah, sure," I said. "Oh, we gave a ride to this kid named Warrior."

"That's a funny name," Isa Faye said. "Can't wait to hear all about it. Are y'all coming back tomorrow?"

"Don't know yet. Funeral's tomorrow afternoon." I didn't want Isa Faye to know I didn't plan to come back at all. I could hear the air rushing through the telephone line, and I had to change the subject to keep from getting all watery eyed. "Las Vegas is something. You wouldn't believe it. Why, Warrior says Mr. Stiletto looks just like Wayne Newton!"

"Oh my gosh, that little kid that sings 'Danke Schoen' on TV?"

"I guess. Tell Mr. Hamilton I said hello, okay?"

"I will. We miss you."

"Guess I better go."

"We love you, Harlan. You travel safe now."

"'Bye."

A hollow feeling grabbed hold of me as I put down the receiver, and for a minute I felt real homesick. But I pushed my feelings away. I was never going home.

Paps was waiting when I got back outside. He studied the ground pretty hard as we walked back to the station wagon and didn't say anything. He didn't even ask about the Hamiltons.

"Anybody for downtown?" Warrior asked. "You guys should see a little bit of Las Vegas while you're here." He unlocked the station wagon and helped me flip up the backseat.

The idea of going downtown lifted my spirits. "I'd love to see all those lights," I said. "They say it's as bright as day."

Paps sat in the front passenger seat. "We could drive around some, but tomorrow is going to be busy, and we need to get some dinner and check into the motel." He held his Bible in his lap. "Warren, I do not want to just leave you here on your own. Come stay with us tonight. You can look around tomorrow afternoon while we attend the funeral. Maybe get some leads on work."

"That would be great, Reverend," Warrior said. "I really appreciate it." Warrior backed the station wagon down the drive of the funeral home.

We headed to downtown. The sun had almost set and the lights glowed against the pink and baby-blue sky. We drove up Las Vegas Boulevard, and a sign about the size of the state of Oklahoma advertised Elvis was playing at the Hilton. I wanted a postcard of the neon cowboy welcoming us to Las Vegas, but

Paps wouldn't let Warrior park the car.

Downtown Las Vegas was bright as daylight. Warrior drove slow through the traffic, and every slot machine at the Horseshoe Casino glittered through the glass to the street outside. People meandered about, talking and laughing. One old man counted a fat wad of money.

Grandfather's smiling face popped into my head, and I understood why he was so happy. Who wouldn't be happy in Las Vegas? Just past the Horseshoe, two good-looking blondes waved at us and blew a kiss at Warrior. I gave a small wave back on the sly.

That was enough for Paps. "This place is nothing but evil," he said. "Warren, drive on to the motel now. We have seen enough."

Maybe *we* had. But *I* sure as hell hadn't.

"We cannot keep the money." Paps scooped egg with his soggy toast. "That money is tainted with sin, Harlan Q, and there is no way to justify it for the Lord."

It wasn't even seven o'clock in the morning, and there we sat in a back booth of the motel coffee shop with cleaned plates and two cups of steaming coffee. Paps had probably fretted all night about the money, then dragged me out of bed just to tell me it was a no go.

"So you're just going to forget about the radio show?" I asked.

"You heard what Mr. Crook told us about my father. He ran a *bar*. It was money made by selling alcohol—to desperate sinners looking for salvation in the bottom of a glass."

"What about the Eldorado?" I asked.

"That car is nothing more than a sin wagon," Paps said. He leaned forward. "Cars like that do nothing more than attract easy women."

And what was so bad about that?

"We will just have to think of some other way to get the money for the radio show." Paps stirred his coffee. "We have got to walk away from it all, Harlan. The money. The Eldorado. All of it. The Lord is testing us."

"Do whatever you want, Paps," I said. "But why did you drive Grandfather all the way out here if you didn't plan to keep the money?"

"It was never my plan. It was the Lord's," Paps said. "You know, we had great hopes for this trip, Harlan, that you would find God and take your place in our ministry. Even yesterday, we saw the power of the Lord working on you, and we were so close. So close . . ."

". . . but no cigar?" I blurted out.

An unyielding pain crossed Pap's face. "We know the Lord must have another plan for you, Harlan," he said. "We cannot know the mind of God. But we do know this money was made from the misery of others, and we cannot ride on the coattails of sin, not even for the radio show."

"Fine." I flipped my spoon through my fingers and neither one of us spoke. "Burn the money, I don't care. I'm sure the church deacons will appreciate what a goody-goody you are."

Paps ignored my sarcasm. "The Lord opens doors and closes them, Harlan." He smoothed his perfect hair. "We will just need to look for another open door that does not include the money. . . ."

Jesus, God, Mary, and Joseph, it hit me like a ton of bricks. Grandfather's inheritance money. Paps didn't want it. And if he didn't want the money, it wouldn't be stealing if I took it. Would it?

". . . We cannot covet money from weak-willed fools who look for help and happiness in the bottom of a bottle. We have to give it away. Pray with me, son."

"Right here in the coffee shop?"

Paps bellowed out into the morning. "Dear Lord, oh gracious Lord, forgive these pitiful men and women who turn away from You to find joy in sin and degradation. . . ."

The counter was full of red-eyed men and women who didn't seem like praying types. A middle-aged couple at the next table turned to look at us.

". . . .who feed their addictions to drink and gamble so they can feel better about their small, insignificant lives."

Half the coffee shop was staring at us. The waitress gave me a dirty look. I slouched down into the booth and poured sugar into my coffee cup. I should get a million dollars just for having to sit here with Paps.

"We pray that they turn to You, dear Father, to mend their miserable lives where there is no real hope, no real harmony, no real happiness. Forgive them, Father. They know not what they do. We are Your humble servants, now and for all eternity. Praise Your name, amen."

By that time, I had poured about sixteen teaspoons of sugar into my coffee.

The waitress ripped the check out of her book and waved it in front of Paps. "I'd watch that mouth of yours, mister," she said. She slapped the paper onto the table.

I knocked my spoon around the edge of my coffee cup and hoped maybe I would just disappear.

"It is settled then," Paps said. "We need to head home as quick as we can. Las Vegas is just pure evil." He stood up. "God is working on your soul, Harlan. Praise be, it will not be long." Paps took the check to the cash register.

I took a sip of my hot coffee, and the taste of sugar burned on my tongue.

The middle-aged man next to us glared at me again. "Weirdos," he said.

There was nothing—not one blasted thing—fair about Paps. I didn't come all the way out to Las Vegas for Paps to give away one swell purple Eldorado convertible and fifty thousand dollars. That money was mine. It was my ticket to get the hell away from Paps.

Paps went to buy a newspaper across the street at the Quik Shop, and I went back to the room. Warrior was up. He was completely dressed, sitting cross-legged in the middle of his bed.

"Just finished my morning meditation," he said. "Where's the Reverend?"

"Getting a newspaper." I flopped down on the bed.

"Hey, why don't we go look around a little?" Warrior said. "The Reverend left me the car keys."

"We have to hurry before Paps gets back," I said. "He's all freaked out about Las Vegas."

"Then just write him a note," Warrior said. "We'll be back by eleven—we can beg his forgiveness then."

I was up and looking for a pen before Warrior could find his shoes. This was perfect. I could talk to Warrior and make my plans. I found a tiny pad of paper by the phone and wrote Paps a note:

Went with Warrior. Back soon. HQ.

"Hurry up. Paps won't be that long."

Warrior and I were unlocking the station wagon when I saw Paps across the highway.

"Let's go to Long Gone Daddy's," I said.

"Your grandfather's bar?"

"It's on East Charleston, near downtown someplace. We'll find it."

"Okay," Warrior said. "It's probably not open, but we can drive by."

I rolled down the window and then switched on the radio. The wind whipped my hair into a frenzy as Janis Joplin sang "Me and Bobby McGee" in a craggy voice raw from whiskey and cigarette smoke. Next to Jimi Hendrix, old Janis was pretty cool. She sang from her soul, and it kind of made my heart hurt. Janis had it right. I had nothing to lose.

Long Gone Daddy's was closed. We found it at the back of a strip shopping center, with only a tiny sign. Someone had hung a black ribbon on the door. The whole place oozed a small-town feeling that wasn't like Las Vegas at all. The bar could have been smack-dab in the middle of Bean's Creek.

"You want to go up and try the door?" Warrior said. "I don't think anybody's around."

"Well, let's try it anyway. There's a car in the back." We parked the station wagon by the back door and knocked hard. No answer. Finally, I pulled the door, and it opened. "Hello?" I yelled. "Hello!"

"Hey!" A voice from inside sounded. "We're closed until three."

The inside of the place was darker than midnight, and it wasn't much bigger than Isa Faye's kitchen. A pool table filled the back of the room, while a bar stretched down one side. Tiny tables lined up along a worn red carpet, and an old jukebox sat solid in the corner. A middle-aged woman—near as I could tell—stood behind the bar.

"We're closed until three today. The owner of the bar died of a heart attack. Can't serve you boys now. But come back this afternoon. We're planning on partying in honor of the boss."

She eyed us in the darkness. "How old are you, anyway?"

"Not old enough to be in here, I reckon," I said. "But the owner of the bar was my grandfather. I just wanted to see the place."

"So you're Harlan Q?" the woman asked.

"Yes, ma'am."

"Well, I'll be. Your granddaddy talked about you. Come sit at the bar."

Warrior and I pushed stools up to the tall counter and sat down. "This is my friend, Warrior," I said. "My father and I are here for the funeral this afternoon, but he's busy. I just wanted to see Long Gone Daddy's."

"Well, here it is. The original. I guess it's a Las Vegas landmark of sorts." The woman was stocky and had shoulders about as broad as Dallas quarterback Roger Staubach. She had short blue-black hair and wore dark eyeliner and red lipstick. Long painted nails reached out to me to shake my hand.

"Harlan Q. Stank," I said.

"Warren Ducklo. Friends call me Warrior." Warrior shook her hand.

"Dee Ray Carr. Nice to meet you. Ever been in a bar before, Harlan?"

"No, ma'am."

"A virgin, then." Dee Ray grinned at Warrior. "Want a drink? It's against the law and all, but there are special circumstances."

Warrior raised his eyebrows. "Got a breakfast beer?"

"The house specialty is a Red Draw—tomato juice and

beer with a dash of Tabasco. How 'bout one of those?" Dee Ray said.

"I'll have just a beer—whatever beer's handy," Warrior said. "Not much on tomato juice."

Dee Ray slid back the top to a refrigerated cooler. She pulled a brown-glass bottle out of the ice, flipped the top with a bottle opener, and handed it to Warrior. Then she opened one for herself.

"How about you, Harlan?"

Paps would be laid out right along with Grandfather if he knew I was in a beer joint. "Did my grandfather drink?" I said. "I mean, we never met or nothing, so I don't know much about him."

"He was a whiskey-and-Coke man. Want one of those?"

"Whiskey and Coke it is," I said. I wished Isa Faye and Mr. Hamilton were here. And Grandfather, too. We could all sit around and talk and laugh.

Dee Ray filled a glass with ice and poured the dark brown liquor into the glass. "We'll make it a light one," she said. She poured Coke into the ice and stirred it with a thin red straw. "I'll even put a cherry in it for good looks." Dee Ray sat the drink in front of me.

"Well, here's to Grandfather," I said. It seemed like they were always toasting something or somebody on TV. I had always wanted to do that. Dee Ray tapped the edge of her beer on the rim of my glass.

"Cheers," Warrior said.

"Cheers." Dee Ray clinked her beer bottle with Warrior,

and she and Warrior both took long swigs.

I slugged down a gulp of my whiskey and Coke, then spit out nearly half of it all over Warrior. Whiskey tasted a lot like battery acid. The Coke just made it taste like sugary battery acid. I swallowed hard and felt the whiskey burn down the back of my throat.

"You okay?" Warrior asked, wiping my drink off his shirt.

"Fine," I said in a whisper. "Just fine." I coughed. "So, here we are. Right here at Long Gone Daddy's."

"Well, it don't look like much, but it's been a good home to a lot of people along the way," Dee Ray said. "I come here about ten years ago, needing a job, and Harlan O hired me without so much as batting an eyelash. You know, he left me the bar in his will?"

I didn't know. But that seemed all right with me. I liked old Dee Ray.

"Speaking of jobs," Warrior said. "Got any openings? I want to stay on here in Las Vegas for a while. I'm a hard worker. Honest."

"You twenty-one?"

"Almost," Warrior said.

"Well, depending on what happens, we might need a bar back to help out—you know, somebody to help set up and clean up. You don't make drinks or sell any alcohol, but it's steady work, and everybody pretty much shares tips and such. But it's dirty work, and you gotta work nights."

Warrior nodded. "I could do that."

"As cute as you are, you sure couldn't hurt business any,"

Dee Ray winked at Warrior. "I could let you know in a couple of days." Dee Ray turned to me. "Like your whiskey and Coke?"

"It's tasty," I lied. "I can't even taste the whiskey at all."

Dee Ray smiled a wide-open smile. "Want to play the jukebox?" Dee Ray slapped a quarter on the counter. "It's two plays for two bits. Your grandpa always played K-16."

I went over to the jukebox and ran my finger along the play list. K-16. It was a Hank Williams song: "I'm a Long Gone Daddy." I slipped the quarter into the box and punched K-16 and L-28, "Me and Bobby McGee" again.

"Your grandfather named the bar after that song," Dee Ray said. "He said that Hank knew more about people than any head shrink who ever lived."

"Did my grandfather ever say why he came to Las Vegas?" I asked.

"Not directly. But Las Vegas is full of people who wander in and out. Harlan O just seemed to be at home here."

I sat down at the bar again. "He talked about us? I mean, my father and me?" I was almost afraid to ask. Maybe he didn't care a flip for family.

"Hold on," Dee Ray said. She hunted around underneath the bar until she pulled out an old scrapbook. She wiped it off with a dishcloth. "He subscribed to the *Bean's Creek Weekly Gazette.* That's what it's called, right? Kept up with the news and clipped pictures and such out and pasted them in here. Take a look."

I opened the book to the first page. Grandfather had kept

every scrap of my life laid out right there. My name underlined in a list of birth announcements from the McKinney Regional Hospital. A yellowed clipping of my baby picture was taped next to it. I had seen that same photo in the baby book that Mother kept in the attic. There was my first-grade field trip to the Fort Worth Zoo, with my name underlined in red and a circle drawn around my face. There was a picture of my Little League baseball team, The Curios. There was me dressed as Peter Pan from the annual Bean's Creek Halloween Parade— not one of my shining moments. There was me smiling at my eighth-grade graduation. I wished I'd worked hard enough to give Grandfather something really good. There was not one honor-roll list. Not one home run.

Dee Ray interrupted my thoughts. "Talked about y'all every day of his life. I think his only regret was that he never got to know you."

"He said that?" I asked.

"Oh, here," Dee Ray said. "I've got a picture your grandfather always kept on the cash register. I'll give it to you. Cute picture."

Dee Ray handed me a wrinkled photo. Paps couldn't have been more than two or three. Grandfather was dressed up like Santa Claus, and Paps was crying his head off. I grinned and showed it to Warrior.

"Probably need to get going soon," Warrior said.

I sipped on my drink. After two or three swallows, I let the whiskey and Coke just slide down my throat. The battery acid didn't taste so awful now, and I kind of liked the warm burn in my chest. Mother's fruit tea could use some of this stuff. I pulled the cherry off its stem and chewed on it.

"You said Grandfather was a good man? Did he go to church much?"

"Not a churchgoer that I knew," Dee Ray said.

"Was he a gambler?" Warrior asked.

"Rumor was he made pretty good money down at the D. I."

"The D. I.?"

"Desert Inn." Dee Ray restocked beer bottles into the cooler. "Played poker."

"Gambling?" I asked. That's all Paps needed to hear.

"Poker's legal in Nevada," Dee Ray said. "No harm done."

I finished off my drink. "Well, so much for being a virgin."

Dee Ray grinned at me and held out her hand. "It was a pleasure, Mr. Harlan. I'll see you later." She held on to my hand for a moment. "Nice meeting you, Warrior."

"Thanks for the beer," Warrior said. "I'll check back about the work."

I slipped the picture into my shirt pocket. "Thanks," I said. I took one last look around. There was just something about the place. A guy could just sit on a barstool and play the jukebox and be happy. Now that was heaven.

On the way back to the motel, all the buildings on the Strip seemed to sway just a little. Maybe whiskey didn't exactly agree with me. But it sure got my courage up.

"Warrior, you said you ran away when you were my age?" I asked.

"Sure did," Warrior said.

"Why did you go back home?" I leaned my head on the back of the seat.

"Because I was just running. I didn't know where or why. After a while, it seemed like I was spinning in a circle. I ended up cold, tired, and hungry."

"Do you think that would happen to me, too? If I ran away?"

"It wouldn't surprise me," he said. "You toying with the idea of heading out?"

"It's crossed my mind." The whole car felt like a merry-go-round. "Particularly if you would let me crash with you here for a couple of weeks. Just until I get things going. I wouldn't be any trouble. You would never even know I was around. I'd be real . . ."

"No way, Harlan. Can't do it, man."

"But why not?"

"Because it won't solve anything," Warrior said.

I looked away.

"Hey, I know what I'm talking about!" He pulled into the motel parking lot. "Harlan, you can't just run *away*. You got to run *to* something." He stared at me so hard I could feel his eyes on the back of my head. "What do you want, man?" he finally asked.

The parking lot did a spin around the world and then stopped. "I don't know." But the words popped out of my mouth before I could think. "Excitement. Love. Everything!" My face warmed up in embarrassment. I looked out the window and wished to heaven I hadn't gone and run my mouth.

"I want to be just like my grandfather," I said. "Except I'm not going back in twenty years. I'm not ever going back."

CHAPTER
17

"Your daddy was such a sweetie! Such a sweetie!" The woman had big blonde hair and droopy earlobes with heavy gold earrings. She kissed Paps, and a red-lipped tattoo branded his cheek.

By the time Warrior dropped us off at the Hopewell Chapel, there was already a hundred people waiting in line. The family visitation had been scheduled prior to the service, and Paps and I had stood shaking hands and smiling with total strangers for the better part of an hour.

The crowd included a Nevada state legislator, a lounge singer from the Golden Nugget, various pit bosses from the D. I., a genuine Elvis impersonator, a couple of off-duty policemen, and a whole crew of retired truck drivers, used car salesmen, various pawnbrokers, and good-looking waitresses. Dee Ray was there, and she shook hands with Paps but never let on that she had already met me.

"It pains us to know that our own father associated with charlatans and two-bit gamblers," Paps whispered to me during a break. "Worse than some criminal."

"Good Lord, Paps," I said. "Jesus hung out with characters a lot worse than Grandfather."

"How many times do we have to remind you about the Lord's name in vain, Harlan?"

"Do you know where the restroom is?" I decided to change the subject.

"Around the corner." Paps's eyes narrowed. "But do not go wandering around. We do not need any more sightseeing today."

I hadn't exactly told Paps the truth about Long Gone Daddy's. I found the bathroom, finished my business, and washed my hands. My cowlick stood straight at attention, so I flicked some water on it and tried to rake it down with my fingers. When I leaned over to get a cold drink from the water fountain, Paps's baby picture with Grandfather slipped out of my Sunday-shirt pocket onto the floor. I had kept it to show Paps, but not now. Not with him calling Grandfather a criminal.

I took my seat in the chapel. Most of the mourners had settled into their chairs. Yellow roses covered Grandfather's casket, and there were all kinds of flowers and wreaths in the chapel. My nose twitched a little from the perfume of it all. A cassette tape played a harmonica version of "Red River Valley." Paps was set to give the sermon, but he was still standing out in the hall talking to the Crook sons.

Someone touched my shoulder. Mr. Stiletto sat down beside me. "My condolences about your grandfather, kid," he said. "Maybe after this is all over, I can take you over and show you some of your grandfather's old haunts. The D. I. was like a second home to him."

"Wow, you'd take me to the Desert Inn?"

"You know the D. I.?" Mr. Stiletto stared at me for a second.

"I just guessed," I said. "D. I.—Desert Inn."

Mr. Stiletto smiled slightly, and for some reason, goose bumps ran down both my arms, but it wasn't cold in the room. Mr. Stiletto turned in his chair and read the program.

Hard to believe Grandfather was a gambler. I closed my eyes and a picture of thousands of twenty-dollar bills filled my eyelids. *Thou shall not steal.* Between outright lying and taking the Lord's name in vain, I figured me and the Commandments were pretty much upside down. I still didn't like the idea of outright stealing, but Paps didn't want the money, and Mr. Stiletto couldn't make Paps take it. So, in a way, I was doing them both a favor. Right?

Paps came in and sat beside me, and the funeral service began. Not one person spoke about sin or Hell or meeting anybody at the river. The funeral offered no formal hymns. No prayers. No amens. No big crying even. They just told stories about Grandfather. Told jokes about Grandfather meeting J. Edgar Hoover at the Pearly Gates, and teased about who had custody of Harlan O's famous Red Draw recipe.

Paps stood up and coughed into his hand when it was time for the sermon. He took his Bible and stood at the podium, looking at us for a long time without speaking. The mourners probably thought Paps was all grief stricken. He wasn't. I had seen that look. He was standing there sizing up every soul in the room, figuring out who might take the walk to Jesus.

"My father was a character." Paps's voice boomed out over the chapel. "You people have told stories today about just what a real character he was. A barkeep. A gambler. A man who liked other people—but liked himself pretty well, too. But what you all have missed is that he was a man. And a sinner. And at this very moment, as we sit here and joke and remember all the good times we had with Harlan O, my father's soul—right this very minute—is in Hell doomed to eternal fire and anguish, and that is the life and death he chose."

A bitter taste came up from my throat.

"My father never met his Lord." Paps had this kind of rabid-dog look in his eyes. "He never attended church. He never prayed. He never gave up his habits of drinking and smoking and gambling. He never got down on his knees and asked for God's forgiveness. Never. Not one time in all the years I was growing up. And if I went around the room, none of you would be able to recollect my father's personal relationship with his Lord."

I studied my program and tried not to look at Paps. Mr. Stiletto looked at his watch and readjusted his chair.

Paps went on and on and on. "So that brings us here." Paps paused in the quiet. "To this chapel to tell stories about my father. Well, those stories were humorous, loving even, but they cannot save my father's soul. And they cannot save yours, either."

Mr. Stiletto shifted again in his chair; our eyes caught in a glance. I felt the heat rising off my face.

When Paps finished preaching, nobody answered the call of the Lord. Paps stood at the podium and flicked his ear a couple of times. Chairs creaked and a few people coughed. No takers.

The cassette player started up again, with "Deep in the Heart of Texas." Paps sat down without looking up, and Crook and his sons took their places at Grandfather's casket. Mr. Stiletto leaned over me and spoke to Paps. "This next part is a little tradition from your father's bar. You don't mind, do you?" He didn't even wait for Paps to blink.

Mr. Stiletto stood up and faced the crowd. "I was an old friend of the departed, as many of you in this room were. So, boys and girls, there's only one thing left to do," he said. "Say good-bye to the best barkeep and cardplayer in the desert. Ready?"

A few hollers in the back of the chapel said "Wait," but Mr. Stiletto held out a deck of cards in front of him. "Godspeed, Harlan O! Godspeed! One, two, three . . . Salute!"

Hundreds of playing cards soared through the room, catching the air like tiny airplanes. They burst from the hands of the mourners in a kind of fifty-two-card pickup game that left the whole chapel covered in queens and jacks and jokers. Diamonds and spades, hearts, and clubs were sprinkled on the casket. It was magic.

Seeing all those cards free in the air made me smile. I sure wished Grandfather could have been there.

Paps glared at Crook and his sons. I could tell he was about to go ballistic. I grabbed two playing cards that had flown into my lap and stood up. Crook nodded, and the casket was wheeled down the aisle to the double doors. Paps followed behind Grandfather.

When we got outside, Paps hurried on in the heat to the

gravesite, but I tried to keep my distance. I didn't want to be around Paps.

Stiletto followed close behind me. "Jesus, Harlan Q, do you suppose Hell is any hotter than Nevada in August?" He grinned. His cowboy hat shaded his face.

I looked down at the cards in my hand. Both of them were queens of hearts. What were the odds that two queens of hearts would fall right into my lap?

"You got lucky cards, kid," Mr. Stiletto said. "That's a sure sign you're Harlan's grandson. He was the luckiest son-of-a-gun cardplayer I ever met."

I looked down at the ladies in my hand. Was Grandfather trying to tell me something from the grave?

"You coming with the preacher over to the office?" he asked.

I nodded.

"See you later then," he said. "Keep those cards close now."

Excitement skipped all over me. Paps made some lame appeal for Grandfather's soul while I held onto my cards until they were damp from my own sweat. Did Grandfather send me those cards for encouragement?

Soon as Grandfather was lowered into the grave, Paps looked down and nodded. "Warren should be here in about ten minutes. We need to go on over to Mr. Stiletto's office, take care of our business, and be out of this godforsaken place."

"Okay," I said, but I didn't rush to get back to the chapel, even though it was about 110 in the shade. I shook some more hands and thanked people for coming out. Mr. Stiletto nodded at me and tipped his hat. People drifted down the sidewalk until I was alone. Paps was already at the chapel door waiting for me, but I took one last look at Grandfather's casket and slipped my thumb over the cards in my hand until the two queens smiled out at me.

"I got you here all safe and sound so you can have a good old rest now, Grandfather," I said. "Now I got a favor."

A woman's laughter drifted up from the parking lot. I showed Grandfather the cards. "Could you use whatever connections you got to help get hold of that inheritance money?" I asked. "I just need a little luck. You understand, don't you?" I waited for a minute, but there was no sign. Grandfather kept his secrets.

I rubbed those two cards together and dropped them into the grave. They glided into the earth like tiny magic carpets and landed light as feathers on the casket, both staring straight up at me, hearts shining. I took that as good as a wristlock handshake.

"Thanks, Grandfather."

"Harlan!" Paps called to me from the sidewalk. "Warren telephoned just now. The station wagon has broken down at a gas station somewhere downtown. We will have to get a ride with Mr. Stiletto to his office."

I looked one more time into Grandfather's grave. The lucky ladies smiled back at me. That money was as good as mine.

CHAPTER

18

"When we get to the office, you can call the service station," Mr. Stiletto said. "The will shouldn't take two shakes, if you know what I mean. It's plain and simple."

The backseat of Mr. Stiletto's Mark IV was bigger than my whole room at the Hamilton's and smelled like leather and Brute cologne. For a minute, I imagined myself some VIP, big-dogging it around Las Vegas, but reality set in pretty quick.

"We have decided not to accept the inheritance money," Paps said.

"You're a funny guy, Reverend." Mr. Stiletto glanced back at me. I was sure he was thinking the *we* was me, too. Wrongo pongo.

Paps stared out the passenger seat window. "That money was made through drinking and gambling, and we do not condone that kind of behavior. No offense, Mr. Stiletto, but we are simple people trying to live the word of the Lord. That inheritance money is sin money, and we just cannot accept it."

"Well, I can't help you there." Mr. Stiletto pulled into a parking lot, next to a small square building. He eased the car into a parking spot and cut the engine. "You're the heir, like it or not, and my job is to administer the will. I have a cashier's check made out to you in the office, so the fifty thousand dollars is yours."

Paps didn't say anything. He opened the car door and the heat of the concrete rushed in, and everything was left up in the air.

It was then I saw it. At the end of the row sat a 1972 deep purple Eldorado convertible. A knockout! "Holy smokes! Is that Grandfather's car?" My voice shot upward in excitement until I sounded like Tiny Tim's sister. I coughed as loud as I could to cover up my changing voice, but Mr. Stiletto chuckled.

"As a matter of fact, it is. Brand-spanking new." Mr. Stiletto opened his car door. "Maybe we'll have time for a quick once around the block when I'm finished here. No problemo, right, Reverend?" But I got the feeling that Mr. Stiletto didn't care much if Paps minded or not.

I ran over to the Eldorado. It was purple, all right, with chrome wheels and a white ragtop. The bright sunlight reflected off the window, so I hooded my eyes with my hands. The inside was deep-purple velvet with a rich, wood-grain dash. I could just see myself driving this car right down the Las Vegas Strip with two or three showgirls keeping me company. Lord, have mercy!

Paps called from the front door of the building as Mr. Stiletto unlocked the door. "Come on, Harlan Q. We do not have time for this foolishness."

It was only about seven seconds of foolishness, for God's sake. I popped the handle and about blistered my fingers on the sun-seared chrome. The door was locked. I shaded my eyes again.

"Harlan Q!" Paps sounded irritated. That made two of us.

Inside, Mr. Stiletto's office was freezing cold and a mess of paper. Stacks of files covered the floor until the large office seemed tiny.

"Pardon my mess," Mr. Stiletto said. "Business is a killer, if you know what I mean. We'll sit at the table." He cleaned off a section of a glass-topped table surrounded by fat green leather chairs. "I'll explain the assets of the estate, and we'll get this all tidied up. Won't take long at all. Can I get you a glass of water? I guess I shouldn't offer you a drink."

Paps just stood there in his saggy tan suit hugging his Bible. "Water," he said. Mr. Stiletto disappeared but returned with three puny juice glasses only half filled.

"Here we go. Sit down, sit down," he said.

I reached for a glass, but Mr. Stiletto waved my hand away. "Don't want to get these mixed up, kiddo." He took the glass nearest him and downed it in one pass, then slid the other two juice glasses to me. "Cool, clear water," he said, then he winked. I pulled out a chair and sat next to Paps.

"If we could get on with this, please," Paps said. He laid his Bible on the table next to him.

Mr. Stiletto talked to me. "Maybe you won't be too bored with all this," he said.

Paps cleared his throat.

Mr. Stiletto opened his file and rummaged through several sheets of paper. "Okay, the cash inheritance is fifty thousand, forty-seven dollars, and twenty-six cents made out to Harlan Stank in the form of a cashier's check," he said. "I failed to add your middle initial, but, you know, I think it will be fine."

What? If the check was made out to Paps without his middle initial, then the check was made out to me, too. Grandfather was working overtime.

"Just sign this release, and I'll surrender the check to you, Reverend," Mr. Stiletto said.

"But what if we do not want the money?"

Mr. Stiletto didn't even flinch. "You still got to accept the check, Reverend. Do whatever you want with the cash from there."

Paps let out a long sigh. "Do you know how much of this money was made through drinking and gambling?" he asked Mr. Stiletto.

"No idea," Mr. Stiletto said. "Money doesn't exactly have a conscience."

I looked at Paps. "You can always give it to charity when we get back to Bean's Creek," I said.

"We suppose we could let the church deacons decide how to dispense with it," Paps said.

"Whatever makes you happy, Reverend." Mr. Stiletto handed the pen to Paps.

Paps wiped his hand along his mouth and sat quiet for a long time. He flicked his ear. He stared at the table. Finally, he sighed a sound of defeat. "We will accept it, then," he said. "Where do I sign?"

"Here and here," Mr. Stiletto said.

I was one step closer to getting away from Paps.

"Here's the cashier's check made out to Harlan Stank." Mr.

Stiletto handed Paps a long white envelope. He grinned at me. "Now don't leave the kid here in charge of that check," he said. "Without that initial, it's made out to him, too, not that that's a problem."

Paps put the check in his Bible. Neither one of us smiled.

Mr. Stiletto continued. "I also have the title to the Eldorado, which needs to be signed over to you, Reverend. Again, there is a release form. The car can be shipped to you in Texas or you can elect to drive it back. I would assume you want it shipped?"

"Could we just sell it here?" Paps asked.

"You could give it to me!" I said.

Mr. Stiletto chuckled, but Paps frowned. "Harlan, you do not even drive. We could give it away to some needy family, we suppose."

Paps signed the forms.

"You can ship the car to Bean's Creek? Will that be expensive?"

"Not too terrible," Mr. Stiletto said. He pulled another sheet of paper out of his file. "Your father left his bar, Long Gone Daddy's, to a former employee, a gal named Dee Ray Carr. I'm guessing that's fine with you?" Mr. Stiletto asked. "No ambitions, there, hey, Reverend?"

Paps jerked back like he had been slapped. "None," Paps said in his most righteous voice. "We do not even wish to visit that evil place. We can only imagine it is Hell on Earth."

No way. I knew what Hell was. It was being the Sunnyside Savior's Reverend Harlan P. Stank's son. That was Hell. Long

Gone Daddy's was about the best place in the world.

"Your old man stipulated that his personal effects be sold. Do you want to go through any of your father's personal items?"

"No," Paps said in a hard voice. "Not at all."

Didn't Paps want to know anything about Grandfather? Paps didn't care for nothing.

"We'll send you a check, then, to settle up," Mr. Stiletto said. "You may want to . . ."

"Fine," Paps interrupted him. "You handle the details. We need to get back to Bean's Creek, so we would like to wrap this up as soon as possible. If you do not mind, we need to call Warren to check on the station wagon."

Mr. Stiletto closed his file. "A little anxious? Well, that takes care of most of the will, anyway. I'll make copies of everything and mail them to you. There is a phone at the receptionist's desk you can use. I'll show you."

Mr. Stiletto showed Paps the phone, but I just sat rocking back and forth in my chair, staring at the tip of the envelope. I could take the check out of the envelope and Paps would probably never know it was missing. This was too easy.

I heard Paps talking on the phone. I leaned over and fingered the cover of Paps's Bible, then checked closer to see if the envelope was sealed, but Mr. Stiletto came back into the room. I jumped back into my chair until it almost tipped over backwards into a stack of files.

"Careful," Mr. Stiletto said. "I think I'm giving you a ride over to the service station. Maybe we can drive the Eldorado?

I'll check with your father as soon as he's off the phone."

"Thanks," I said. I tried to change the subject. I didn't want Mr. Stiletto guessing what I was up to. "Did my grandfather know any gangsters? Like guys in the Mob?" I asked.

"This is Las Vegas," Mr. Stiletto said. "What do you think?"

"I bet he knew plenty of them."

"Maybe a few." Mr. Stiletto straightened out the papers and then picked up his folders. Paps was still yakking in the other room. "So, your old man been a minister a long time?"

"Sort of."

"You plan on following in his footsteps?"

"No, sir. I don't have the gift, exactly."

Mr. Stiletto laughed out loud. "I would guess you are a lot more like your grandfather."

"What was he like?"

"The genuine article," Mr. Stiletto said. "The genuine article."

We heard Paps hang up the phone. "I'll be right back," Mr. Stiletto said.

It was now or never. I flipped open the Bible and ran my hand down the inside front cover. The envelope was made of thick white paper and the flap was tucked in neatly. It wasn't sealed. I heard Paps out in the hall.

All I had to do was open the envelope, take out the cashier's check, and put it in my pocket. It was that simple. I fingered the flap again. Open the envelope! That's all I had to do. Open the envelope! Paps's voice boomed louder. Take the check! Put it in my pocket! Do it! Do it!

But I froze. Something in me choked, and I couldn't move. I wanted to run out the door. I couldn't steal the money! I couldn't. No way in hell. I slammed the Bible shut.

I turned and flung myself away from the table but ran smack dab into Mr. Stiletto standing in the doorway. He had seen the whole business.

A heavy twinge of guilt took hold of me, and I was afraid I might have another hyperventilating fit right there. But Stiletto just looked at me and lifted his index finger to his lips. An ice-cold chill went right up my spine. "Your old man's in the john," he said. "Be out in a minute."

Then, Stiletto backed me up to the table. "Open the Bible," he said. He took another white envelope out of his suit pocket. "Let's just make a little switcheroo, shall we?"

I picked up the Bible and opened the cover. He laid the second envelope next to the spine. "Pick up the check, kiddo, and put it in your pocket."

My throat tightened, and I was afraid to breathe, but I was more afraid to question Mr. Stiletto. Was this an offer I couldn't refuse? I did as I was told. I folded the first envelope and settled it deep in my pocket

I could feel the hot breath of his smile on my face. Mr. Stiletto pressed the Bible closed in my hands. "We all need a little help from our friends," he said.

I tried to catch my breath. Had Grandfather sent Mr. Stiletto to help me? Mr. Stiletto backed away and laid the Bible on the table. "We'll talk a little business directly," he said.

As we walked to the car, Stiletto was cool as a cucumber. I drummed the outside of my pocket and tried to be calm, but I was worse than a cat in heat. If Paps found out that I took the money, he would kill me himself, whether my soul was saved or not.

Just as we got to the Eldorado, Paps opened his Bible and looked right at the bogus envelope. What if he opened it? Mr. Stiletto didn't even flinch. He would let *me* take the rap. I had to think of something fast! Don't God help those who help themselves?

"Paps!" I yelled. There was nothing left to do. I leaned forward and gave it everything I had. I puked all over creation.

CHAPTER

Paps jammed the envelope into his jacket pocket. "Oh, my word! Are you sick, son" Paps said. "Harlan, try not to get it all over your clothes." Paps handed me a handkerchief.

One good gag, and I was done. I bent over and rested my hands on my knees. My tie was the only casualty. The puke wasn't much but Coca-Cola and some old scrambled eggs from breakfast. I spit on the pavement. I had sidetracked Paps. He never even looked at the envelope, and now it was lost in his coat pocket. It would probably be hours before he realized where it was.

Stiletto started the Eldorado and flipped the air conditioning on full blast. "Kid's probably not used to this heat. A cold, wet towel might do him some good. Be right back." Stiletto fumbled with his keys while Paps opened the car and steered me over to the front passenger seat.

"Sorry," I said. Within a minute, Stiletto came back again with some ice, an old grocery bag, and a wet towel. He handed the towel to me, and I washed down my face. "I feel a little better," I said.

"The service station is only about five minutes away," Stiletto said to Paps. "Maybe you should take my car and drive over. It's just down Las Vegas Boulevard."

"Well, we hate to leave you with a sick child. But we do need to see about the station wagon. . . ." His voice trailed off.

"We'll be fine. Go on."

"We planned to start home tonight. Do not be offended, Mr. Stiletto, but we do not care for Las Vegas."

"I'll pass that along to the chamber of commerce," Stiletto said. He handed his keys to Paps. "Just go left out of the parking lot, then take the next right. It's straight down the Strip toward downtown, about five or six blocks. We'll be over in a few minutes."

The second Paps drove out of the parking lot, I felt better.

"Still got the check, kid?"

"It's still in my pocket."

"So what do you plan to do with it?"

"Keep it?"

Stiletto just stared at me.

"Hang out in Las Vegas?"

He still stared.

"Okay. Okay," I said. "I want to get the hell away from my paps. Run away. I need the money . . ."

Stiletto threw his head back and clapped his hands. A deep laugh came up out of his gut. "Can't stand the old man, huh?" he said. "Don't blame you for that one."

I shrugged my shoulders.

"So how are you going to cash the check?" he asked. "It's made out to you, but you're not exactly legal, if you know what I mean."

"I haven't gotten that far," I said. And the truth was, I didn't know. I didn't have any idea. "Why are you so interested?"

Stiletto didn't answer me. He pursed his lips like he was thinking. "Let's take a ride over to the D. I. Maybe we can introduce you around. Find you some cash."

"You would help me out?"

"Sure, and since I'm helping you, maybe you can help me with a little favor," Stiletto said. "You know, you scratch my back, I scratch yours?"

"Okay." I didn't have much choice.

"Then let's go. We can put the top down, if you want. Uncless you're really sick."

"I'm not that sick," I said. I was plenty nervous about scratching anybody's back. What did he want from me? Stiletto put down the top to the convertible, and we headed out. It was hotter than blazes, but God in heaven, I did like riding in that car.

"How did you meet my grandfather?" I asked, almost yelling to be heard over the hot air whipping past us.

"In a card game," Stiletto said. "Your grandfather took six grand off me in one night, but he was nice about it, you know? I liked him." Stiletto glanced over at me. "When did you start having trouble with the preacher?"

"About five minutes after I was born."

Stiletto laughed again. I glanced over at him and took a deep breath. Now that I had stolen the check, I just wanted the money and to be left alone.

Within five minutes, we were at the Desert Inn's back parking lot. There wasn't one thing in that hotel that wasn't covered in gold or velvet or twinkling lights. My eyes wandered all over the place, but Stiletto didn't see a thing but the bar. He ordered a scotch. "What do you want?"

"A whiskey and Coke," I smarted off. But Stiletto nodded and in a heartbeat that's what I was drinking. "You play at the Desert Inn all the time?" I asked, sipping my drink. It didn't taste as bad as I remembered.

Mr. Stiletto's eyes narrowed.

"It was on that business card you gave me. Professional gambler. I just figured you must play here."

"About every week," he said. "Since you know I'm a professional, how 'bout let's talk a little business here, Harlan. You don't mind if I call you just Harlan, do you?"

I didn't mind. At least, I didn't think I minded. The whiskey settled me down some, and I concentrated hard on Stiletto's words.

"There's a poker tournament going on tonight at the hotel. And you've got that nice, fat check right in your pocket. But that check is not one bit of good unless you can cash it. So the way I figure, I can finagle a few things, get you that cash, and you can do something for me."

"What's that?"

"I need a little stake in tonight's game, if you know what I mean."

I didn't know. "A stake?" I asked.

"Five thousand dollars. That gets me in the game."

"But what if I don't want to give you five thousand dollars?"

"Oh, kiddo, I think you do," Stiletto said. "After all, you

stole the money. That's a felony, even in Nevada."

"You made me take the money!"

"I didn't make you do a thing."

I didn't say a word.

"I'm sure you don't want me to share that little news with the hotel security here, do you?" Stiletto took a drink of his scotch. The old cowboy had me nailed.

I shifted in my chair.

"I thought you were my grandfather's friend."

"I was. He's dead," Stiletto said. "Now, want to go cash that check or not?"

Did I have a choice? "Five thousand and that's it?" I asked.

"And we're done," Stiletto said.

I downed my drink.

We headed for one of the casino cashiers. "Let me handle it," Stiletto said. "This girl is an old, old friend of mine. A good friend, if you know what I mean."

I didn't want to know.

Mr. Stiletto leaned in toward the cashier and whispered for a minute or so. The woman huffed out a big breath between smacks of Doublemint. "I ain't no bank, here, Johnny," she said. "Honey, I'd love to give you fifty thousand in cash, you know that, but the pit boss would fire me in a second. I got kids to feed."

The line behind us snaked out into the casino lobby. We had reached a showdown here; the cashier wasn't coughing up the cash, and Johnny Stiletto wasn't exactly making any progress. Maybe she wasn't such a good friend after all.

"Why, baby, we don't even need the cash," he said.

"Yes we do," I said. Stiletto's eyes narrowed into a warning glance.

"Baby, we just need a line of credit so I can get in the game." Stiletto continued. "I'm feeling real lucky, and I'd be happy to spread that luck around, if you know what I mean?"

The cashier tilted her head to one side. "Johnny, if I had a nickel for every time I've heard that from you, I'd be a rich woman. I'll give you five thousand in chips and a line of credit, but take it or leave it because I got a bunch of unhappy customers."

"We'll take it," he said.

"That's not the deal. I want the cash."

"We'll talk about it later, kid," Stiletto said. "I need the check."

"No, sir," I said. I put my hand in my pocket and held onto the check as tight as I could.

"Give us a minute," Mr. Stiletto said to the cashier. He put his arm around my shoulder real tight. Too tight. "Don't mess with me, kid," he whispered. "I promised I'd get you the cash, and I will. But we need to do this my way."

"When do I get my money?" I asked.

"Give me the check," he said. "Now."

I thought he would break my arm. Stiletto might not look like some mobster, but when did a hit man ever look like a hit man? I handed it over.

"Sign here," the cashier said to me. "Johnny, you're supposed to co-sign for the kid. Did you say he was your nephew?"

"Sister's kid. But why don't you just look the other way? I mean it's a cashier's check and all."

"Just this once," she said. "And just make sure you remember your friends, honey," she said. The cashier stamped the check and pushed a wooden box of chips under the teller bars. "Don't be a stranger."

"Why, I always remember my friends, baby," Stiletto said. "Always." He took the chips and grabbed my arm. The next thing I knew we were waltzing past the lobby toward the card room.

"When do I get my cash?" I asked again. He couldn't kill me right in the lobby.

"Look, I'm going to win us both a little spending money, and you're going to wait right here for me like a good boy. Got it?" Stiletto squeezed my arm tighter. "Then you can head out to the wild blue yonder, and we'll just pretend this never happened."

"Some friend of Grandfather's you are."

"Like I said, kid, he's long gone." We turned the corner into the card room. A big tough guy stood at the door, and Stiletto handed our box of chips over to him.

The guy frowned at me. "Where are *you* going?" he said.

"Into the card room to watch my uncle play poker."

"You can't go in there. Got to be eighteen."

"I'm eighteen. Don't I look eighteen? Eighteen years, two months, and ten days."

The tough guy looked uninterested. "You're not eighteen."

"Are you saying I'm lying?"

"That's what I'm saying. You got a problem with that?"

"No. No problem."

"You can sit out there and wait."

Stiletto motioned me out to the lobby. "I won't be that long," he said.

He went to a back table and sat down with several other players. All I could see was his cowboy hat bobbing up and down.

I looked around and found a chair across from the card room entrance. Maybe the tough guy would get busy later, and I could sneak past him.

It was getting late. The car was probably fixed by now, and Paps might even be looking for me. How long did it take to win a little spending money?

I couldn't sit still. I stood up to see, then sat back down. The big guy never moved. I patted my foot on the red carpet a few hundred times, then paced the carpet in front of the card room.

Slot machines pinged out winners from across the room. I sat down again and inspected the arm of my chair. The velvet was worn and dirty. I chewed on a hangnail until it peeled down to the quick. Stiletto's hat wasn't bobbing up and down anymore. The lobby was almost quiet now. I was dead tired. The whiskey had slowed me down.

Finally, a man wearing big diamonds came out from the card room. The guy at the door smiled and practically fell all over himself lighting the man's cigarette. "That damn Texan is taking everything."

The tough guy laughed. "He's a player. Half crazy, maybe, but one hell of a player."

Texan? From what I saw, Stiletto was the only cowboy in the bunch. The man must be talking about him.

Joy filled my heart, and I have to admit I said a prayer that thanked about every person I had ever known, alive or dead. Of course, Grandfather was at the head of the list. And God was in there, too. I took a deep breath. Everything was going to be okay. I rested my head on the back of the chair and closed my eyes for a minute.

Maybe I could get the cash and live for years in Las Vegas with nobody bothering me. Maybe I could go to work at Long Gone Daddy's someday, and Mr. Hamilton and Isa Faye could come out, and we could go see Elvis at the Hilton. Maybe we could go backstage and Elvis and I would become good pals and ride around in my Eldorado.

Maybe Warrior would become a big movie star, and we would laugh about the old days. Maybe Connie Cleaver would hear about all my success in Vegas and fall madly in love with me, but she'd just have to get in line because I'd have fifteen other girlfriends by then. Maybe I could be happy just like Grandfather had been. Maybe. Maybe. Maybe.

Next thing I knew, I was dreaming all kinds of craziness. I was eating whole coconut cream pies, with me and Paps in an arm-wrestling match.

"Wake up, kiddo." Stiletto gave me a little shove on the arm. "It's time to go home."

"What? Was I dreaming or something . . . ?"

"It's time to get out of here." Tired, dark circles hung under Stiletto's eyes.

"What time is it?" I asked. A nasty film coated the inside of my mouth.

"Almost three a.m. Time to get you back to Long Gone Daddy's."

I yawned into my hand. "I'm not going back there. I just want my spending money you promised. I want my cash. Forty-five thousand, forty-seven dollars, and twenty-six cents."

Stiletto wiped his eyes. "Yeah, yeah. Come on. We'll settle in the car. I can't leave you sitting here all night."

I was awake. "I want my money. You promised you would get me the cash, and I want . . ."

Stiletto shrugged his shoulders. "I lied," he said.

The air stuck in my throat. There was a big mistake here. One hell of a big mistake. "But you said you would get me the money!"

"What a tangled web we weave," Stiletto said, nodding his head. "Kid, that money was mine the minute you handed over the check."

I just stood there like my insides had been pulled out. I wanted to puke all over the place, but I couldn't even manage dry heaves. My head screamed the truth. The money was gone.

"But, hey, let me take you over to the bar. I can't just leave you here. That wouldn't be nice." Stiletto straightened his jacket and tipped back his cowboy hat. "Cheer up, Harlan. It's only money."

Only money. I punched Stiletto in the stomach with everything I had. But he was as strong as an ox and wrestled me into a headlock that about ripped my skull clean off. My head was lodged in the crook of his arm.

He spoke right into my ear, and his breath was hot and smoky. "If you're going to be dumb, kiddo, you got to be tough," he said. "Consider this as just one of life's little lessons, you know what I mean?" Then he let go of me.

I about dropped to the floor but pushed myself back up against the wall. A deep-seated nausea filled my gut, and I gasped the last bits of air in the room. The money was gone. I was damned. God in heaven, I was damned.

I wished I'd never laid eyes on Las Vegas.

CHAPTER
20

A police car sat right next to the front door of Long Gone Daddy's. Stiletto's Mark IV was there, but the station wagon was missing. A neon Open sign flickered yellow into the hot night. Stiletto eased the Eldorado into the parking lot.

"Maybe it's better if we have a parting of the ways here." He flipped the car keys into my lap. "Give these to the preacher." Then he pulled out his wallet. "I'll leave you a little tip," he said. "Always carry an extra key." Stiletto dangled a spare ignition key in the dark, then clutched it in his hand and opened the door.

"Better luck next time," he said. "You know the funny part? Your grandfather never left that money to your old man. He left it to you. But I thought it would be easier to swindle some small-time preacher than rip off a kid's college money. You couldn't have played into my hands any better, kiddo. You and your old man were classic." He slammed the car door.

The money was for me? For college? A sick panic stabbed me in the stomach. "Thanks for nothing!" I yelled. But Stiletto was already cranking up the Mark IV's engine. He was gone.

I was a loser and a screw-up, and that's just the way it was. Even Grandfather couldn't change that.

The front door of Long Gone Daddy's slammed open. "Where have you been?" An accusing rage filled Paps's voice. Warrior followed right behind him, and Dee Ray fretted just outside the doorway.

"Harlan, are you okay?" Warrior asked.

"Get in here. I did not raise a scheming, lying con artist." Paps pulled me in by my collar.

"Let's just take things easy, Reverend," Warrior said. He held his hand up toward Paps. "Come on, Harlan. Man, you had us worried."

Paps pushed harder, and I tripped toward the door. "You made a fool out of me, and you can be assured that there will be punishment for this stupid stunt," he said. "Where have you been? What did you do with that inheritance check, young man? Is it in the car?"

Dee Ray backed up as Paps pushed me forward again, and I banged open the bar door. Warrior and Dee Ray followed behind me. The room was dim and smelled of sour cigarette smoke and detergent.

A policeman sat on a stool, talking on the phone. "No. No. Not this time. Apparently, he showed up on his own."

Warrior nodded outside toward Paps.

"Gotta go." The cop hung up.

"Thanks, man," Warrior said as the cop headed outside.

"The Reverend's in a rage, big time. Harlan, he thinks you took off with some inheritance check. I think you better come clean with him, man."

Dee Ray tried to smile. "I'm just glad you're here, baby. I just knew Harlan O was watching out for you."

Paps burst into the bar and the cop followed. "Answer me

when I ask you a question. Where were you? What did you do with the money? Do not tell me it is in the Eldorado; we just looked." Paps punched his finger into my chest and spit out the words. "What were you trying to pull, Harlan?"

"I was trying to get the hell away from you!" I yelled. I didn't want to give him the satisfaction of knowing that all my dreams had been suckered away by some slick gambler.

"And that justifies stealing?"

"I didn't steal the money. It was mine. Stiletto told me so."

"Lying, too? Look at yourself, Harlan," Paps said. "You are nothing more than a lying thief on a slippery slope."

"It's too late. I'm already damned."

It was as if Paps didn't hear me. "You seem bent on some kind of self-destruction and separation from God. The Lord is trying to save you! Why are you so anxious to see yourself in Hell?"

"Because that's where I belong!" Tears welled up in my eyes, and I spoke fast to keep from crying. "You win. I'm evil. There's nothing you can do about it." I screamed at the top of my lungs. "I can't be some goody-goody Sunday-school son you dream about. I can't stand your preaching and pushing. I can't stand it."

"Take it easy, man," Warrior said.

But I ran at Paps like some crazy-eyed wildcat and slammed him up against the counter and punched and kicked as wild as my strength would let me. "I'm a good-for-nothing doubter, Paps, and God hates my guts," I moaned.

"Oh, my word," Dee Ray said.

Paps didn't fight back. He just held onto me tight as he could. A cry came up from my throat, and I couldn't stop it. In a second, my whole body shook with sobs, but Paps just stood there holding onto me like this was something we did all the time.

"No, no, no, Harlan," he whispered. "Oh, son, God loves you too much. Don't you know that?"

The whole room was real still except for my crying. I didn't care that I was crying in front of Dee Ray, Warrior, and a cop. I didn't care at all.

"Your grandfather's love was shallow." Paps's voice was quiet and sad. "He could give it, or take it, and not think a thing about it. When my mother died, he just turned away. I thought he loved everyone but me, but I had no idea why. Then he just left. Ran for it."

Paps's voice was not more than a whisper. "God's love meant everything to me. And I wanted that kind of love for you, Harlan. So you never had to feel alone . . ." His voice broke a little and he dropped his arms.

I ran my hand over my face to wipe off the tears. "I didn't mean to steal the money, Paps," I said. "But you didn't want it, and I just had to get away somehow. I know I did bad. I know I did. . . ."

"That money means nothing, Harlan. You had to get away? Why?"

I bit the edge of my lip. "'Cause you never loved nothing about me. All you wanted was to save my soul."

"You think I never loved you?" A faint smile crossed Paps's

lips, and he ran his hand over his eyes. "I pray every day for you, son. All I want is love and a spiritual life for you. Maybe I want that too much. But I always love you. Always. No matter what."

His last words were so quiet that I almost didn't hear what he said. But I did hear it. I heard every word of it.

"But what happened to the inheritance money, man?" Warrior said.

"Stiletto stole it," I said.

"What?" Paps asked. "How could that happen?"

"I never trusted that guy," Warrior said.

"I couldn't steal the money when it came right down to it, but Stiletto saw me, and he said I wanted to, but I didn't have the guts. Then he had another envelope, and he made me take the check from your Bible; it was made out to me, no middle initial, remember? Stiletto helped me cash it at the Desert Inn because he wanted to play in some poker tournament and offered to make us both some spending money," I said. "I trusted him. But he lied. He flat-out lied."

"Oh, honey." Dee Ray sat down next to me.

"But I didn't really steal the money. Not really."

Paps looked at me.

"I mean I did, but I didn't. Stiletto told me Grandfather left the money to me for college, but Stiletto let us believe the money was yours. Figured you were an easy target. He conned us both."

"Why did my father ever get mixed up in this place?" Paps said.

"You can't blame Las Vegas, Reverend," Warrior said. "Bad people are everywhere. You just happened to find Stiletto. But a lot of good people here loved your father, and he loved them."

"My father and I never could understand each other. I don't know why we were so very different. But maybe he did find happiness here." For once, Paps didn't seem like a preacher. He was just a regular guy—thrashing around trying to figure stuff out.

"Hey, don't be so hard on yourself," Warrior said. "Let it go, man. You can't change what happened with your old man. But you can change things in the future." Warrior looked at Paps and then at me.

So God didn't have total dibs on love. Grandfather loved Paps. And Paps loved me. And I loved them both, even though I'd never known Grandfather and I couldn't figure out Paps half the time. Love got all jumbled up. But that didn't mean it wasn't there.

The policeman finished his report. "If you want to press charges, we can pick up this Stiletto fellow."

"No, no need," Paps said. "We don't want the money. It was never really ours."

"Okay, then. I guess we're done," the cop said. "Get some sleep," he said. "I know it sounds corny, but it'll be better in the morning."

Paps took his coat off a barstool and looked at me.

I remembered the Eldorado's keys in my pocket. "Here," I said. "Stiletto told me to give you these."

"Well, that is one good thing out of tonight," Paps said. "The engine blew in the station wagon, and we were walking back to Bean's Creek. Guess we can drive the Cadillac, that is, if you are planning to come home?" Paps waited for my answer.

I looked around at the bar. Long Gone Daddy's tugged at me. I would miss it, I knew. But the whole deal with Stiletto had taken the fire out of me. Maybe I wasn't that tough. And now that Paps and I had kind of cleared the air, maybe there was hope for us, too.

Warrior punched my shoulder. "Go on home, Harlan," he said. "Find out what you're running to, man."

I had to admit I'd about had all the fun I could stand. I missed Isa Faye and Mr. Hamilton awful. I missed riding around in the hearse. I missed Mother's chocolate-chip cookies, and I even missed the guys at school. I missed everything about Bean's Creek. Except Breenie. Breenie could just go right on off to Hell.

"Home sounds pretty good," I said. "Hey, Moo Goo, don't forget about me. Let me know when you get to L.A."

"It won't be for a while," Dee Ray said. "Figured we could use some help around here. Warrior's going to work for me. Got a room in the back for him and everything."

"I'll give your phone number to all the showgirls," Warrior grinned. "Just don't break too many hearts."

I hugged Dee Ray's neck. She wrote Long Gone Daddy's telephone number on a beer coaster and gave it to me. "Call me once in a while," she said. "Let me know how you are."

"Good-bye, Warren," Paps said. "Take care of yourself. We'll remember you in our prayers."

"Thanks for everything, Reverend," Warrior said. "I'll see what I can do about selling the station wagon for you. Maybe somebody will want to buy it and fix it up. I won't mention your father." He grinned and pulled Paps into a hug. "I appreciate you letting me go along for the ride," he said. "Never a dull moment with the two of you."

Paps gave Warrior a tired smile. "Don't give up on us," Paps said. "Come see us if you ever get back to Dallas."

"I will. I have something I want to give you, Reverend." Warrior wrote out a telephone number on a paper napkin. "It's my dad's phone number," he said. "He heads up religious programming for First Salvation of Sin Church in downtown Dallas. The radio mission stuff? Maybe he can help you out with your show. Maybe in the whole grand scheme of things, that's why we met in the first place. Maybe it was fate."

"Maybe it was God's will," said Paps. "I will call him and let him know you are a fine young man."

"Thanks, Reverend. Oh, and hey, could you tell him I said hello?"

Paps and I headed out to the Eldorado with our suitcases.

"We can leave the top down," Paps said. "I think I might drive for a while before we stop for some sleep."

I settled into the passenger seat and yawned deep into my chest, then remembered the baby picture of Paps that Dee Ray had given me from the bar. I took it out of my shirt pocket and handed it to him.

"Here," I said. "Dee Ray said Grandfather kept it over the cash register in the bar."

"Who is this with Harlan O?" Paps asked.

"It's you," I said, "when you were a baby. So I guess Grandfather did come back to Bean's Creek to tell us he loved us all along."

Paps didn't say anyhing; he just started the car.

I couldn't stop myself. "For Christ's sake, what's it going to hurt to forgive a dead man? Maybe he wasn't perfect, but Grandfather loved you."

"I told you not to take the Lord's name in vain, Harlan," Paps said.

But then he kind of smiled at me and did something really weird. He cried. Not big old blubbering tears like I had, but tears rolled down his face right as rain. Then he wiped his eyes and looked back at Long Gone Daddy's for a minute before he slipped the picture into his Bible and pulled out of the parking lot.

I turned the radio on low, then leaned back in the seat and watched the lights as we drove south out of town. A sunrise flirted along the dark purple of the desert, and the lights nodded to the morning. The Eldorado skittered down the highway. I looked over at Paps. His hair was flying wild in the wind. We looked good in that car, and I could hardly wait to get home.